As a young boy, Liam B. Dei and his friends had a few games they played together, in empty fields, the things they would do is set traps besides other sports they used to play. To break the boredom of time, they would walk the streets and seek out different schools. All in all, he had a great time with his friends.

These stories are from dreams long past and yet remain in my mind so he thought he would share them with the literary world and find out what is thought about them.

To my childhood friends.

Liam B. Dei

Dumping Grounds

Austin Macauley Publishers™
London • Cambridge • New York • Sharjah

This is a work of fiction. Names, characters, businesses, places, events, locales, and incidents are either the products of the author's imagination or used in a fictitious manner. Any resemblance to actual persons, living or dead, or actual events is purely coincidental.

A CIP catalogue record for this title is available from the British Library.

ISBN 9781528907835 (Paperback)
ISBN 9781528911740 (ePub e-book)

www.austinmacauley.com

First Published 2023
Austin Macauley Publishers Ltd®
1 Canada Square
Canary Wharf
London
E14 5AA

Prologue

"I am the caretaker." He was the owner of the butchery, married; he had always let his wife do as she pleased. He would spend most of his time at work and his wife found ways to entertain herself.

What he had her involved with was the winter club and she did volunteer work with several charities in the community. What he didn't know was she suffered from depression and how she dealt with it was in the casinos. She could spend as much as one hundred thousand dollars in an evening, and it was getting worse.

After selling the butchery, getting ready for retirement he began to go over the finance of his estate and that's when he discovered what was going on with his wife and what she was doing while he was working. She had gone through nine-tenths of the money put into the retirement fund, without his knowledge and he was just now discovering it. After going through the financial debts accumulated by his wife, he came to the discovery that she had put them in debt of more than four hundred thousand dollars. Distraught, he drove down to the building he had just sold and started ranting in disturbed mindlessness.

"I am the caretaker," he said aloud. He was heartbroken, "*What a bitch, I know what I'm going to do, I am the caretaker and I will be here*." As he grabbed the chair after throwing the rope around the support beam, he tested the sturdiness of the rope and stepped onto the chair.

Sliding the rope over his head and around his neck, "If this doesn't get her attention then she is as heartless as I have been saying," he said to himself aloud. Looking around the room, he knew he was in the right place and kicked the chair from beneath him.

Chapter 1

He had just started the job a few months back and thought he had the machine understood. Everything was fine on this day, and he felt good greetings were casual, and everyone was smiling; conversation was light.

"So, how was your weekend?" Vince asked.

"It was great; we were relaxing and having an early morning coffee when we got a flyer inviting everyone to a birthday party at one of the trailers. My wife and I mulled over the idea for about an hour and decided to go. When we got there, we saw that there is a live band, as well as a full BBQ, lay out."

"That's right on," Vince said excitedly.

"Ya, we stayed most of the day and I really didn't know how drunk I was till…."

"Ahhhhhhhhhh…"

"What?"

"My finger" jerry walked over and saw that Vince's finger was dangling from the end joint.

"What did you do?" he questioned as he ran him to the lab, after turning off the printer.

"You need to be taken to the hospital right now."

The people in the lab just looked at the finger and wrapped it in gauze, hurried him out to a waiting car and had him raced to the hospital.

On the way there, they just happen to pass a road speed trap and were then pulled over. Showing Officer Vince's hand with the story of how it happened, he sent them on their way with just a warning.

Getting to the hospital, Vince jumped out of the car before it stopped and went right into Emergency.

He was put ahead of the others waiting, some having been there already two hours.

After looking at his finger, the doctor told Vince that the machine had mangled his finger so bad it couldn't be put back on and would have to be removed. Upset about this Vince began to cry.

"Why it looks like a clean-cut?" Vince exclaimed.

"It is, but the knuckle or joint rather has multiple issues and is irreparable and putting it back on could most likely cause gangrene then we would have to remove the whole hand. Do you want to take that chance?" the doctor questioned.

"Yes," he answered with head down and looking at the floor.

"Okay then; we can sew it surgically, freezing it but this is going to take time so you'll have to stay off work for a few days as well so we can keep an eye on it." He returned to work, ignoring what the doctor said and, reluctantly, taking his meds. Six months went by and he returned to the doctor who then told him that he has a severe infection and if the arm is not removed he would be dead I a few days.

After cleaning the printer, Jerry was about to turn it on when he heard a high squeal come from the boxing packer. "Holy shit, did you hear that, the printer has never done that before? It sounded as though it were laughing. Weird."

"It sounded like it was coming from the auger as well," remarked martin.

"Creepy," they both said in unison.

There was no way they could know; it was I. I use these machines to show I am still here, as well, by moving things around, helping to misplace items and possessions. The butter tray is a heavy piece of iron, though, on wheels, it is still difficult to manoeuvre. I, the caretaker, have the power to move items at will.

To make this happen the moment has to be right, meaning, the people in the area, the room's temperature and the position of the tray has to be in radical indifference to create optimum influence. The floor is uneven, giving a better opportunity to take advantage of; the floor beside the butter boat is perfect, as long as the tray is positioned between the churn and the boat, closest to the north wall or by the water silo, at the mid-floor centred in front of the wrapping machine, is an easy move.

Leslie used Vince as his vice to create incidents, Vince's energy was the best, he is a very angry person and acted out on many different circumstances with "You hate me, I can tell because of the way you talk to me and the way you look at me, you think I'm stupid. Don't you," commenting whenever confronted for being overly aggressive or bashing the machine and swearing out of frustration and anger.

These are the times Leslie chooses to make things happen, he manipulates the wrapper or the boxer into a situation. He is amused by the reactions, and they are always the same. "What the fuck, this fucking thing just can't be right, I want to get a hammer and smash it into being right or till they decide to get a new machine."

Still, for me, it takes forethought, the weight of the tray, with the combined energy of my minion, Leslie, and the energy of who might be in the room can make this happen all the better.

Leslie on the other hand has a way of manipulating objects as well as causing disturbance. For example, the wrapping machine has a problem with tearing, Leslie is the cause of this. He, with one finger, can disturb the paper as it moves through the push fingers to the drop block.

Just by touching the paper with his thumb, Les crates an instant of hesitation to cause tearing. Then blocking the sensor he can keep the machine running and the butter then lines up, unwrapped, for at least twelve pounds. That means the operators have to clean every butter cavity, the belt, the top folding plates and reset the registry. This can, for one person, take a minimum of one hour.

Then there is the pusher on the end of the belt system. Leslie has fun with this one. I can do the larger manipulations, as long as they are on wheels, but Leslie! He has a talent that I cannot master. This is how he turned the boxing pusher onto Vince causing him to lose his finger and eventually the removal of his arm.

Chapter 2
The Interview

Finding himself on the couch again Brent slowly pulls himself up and turned on the weather channel. Scanning the living room he saw that last night's dinner was still sitting on the coffee table, uneaten. Grabbing the dish he got up and took it to the kitchen, setting it on the counter he began the morning ritual of making coffee. Celina came down from the bedroom and in a whispered tone asked, "Can you make breakfast?"

"What would you like?" he interjected.

"You know bacon and eggs."

"It's always the same thing: why can't you think of something more creative or different?"

It was a Saturday morning and the previous night was filled with anxiety and confrontation. Preparing the pan for bacon and setting the coffee maker for the first pot Brent walked to the fridge and pulled out the eggs and started to prepare them to be scrambled. Just then his cell phone rang:

"Hello?"

"Is this Brent?" came a voice from the other end.

"Yes?"

"I'm looking at your resume and I'm wondering if you are available for an interview this week?"

"Yes, I am."

"What day would be good for you?" she questioned.

"Monday is good for me."

"Okay, I have a morning or an afternoon window. What would you prefer?"

"Afternoon would be better for me."

"Okay, I have a 1:30, or a 2 o'clock time period which would you prefer?"

"One thirty would be the best time for me."

"Okay, I'll see you Monday at 1:30, we are at 9666 West Brook."

"Great," setting the cell on the kitchen table he went to the bedroom where Celina was putting on makeup "I have a job interview on Monday."

"Great, this is what I want you to wear."

And she pulled out some clothes from the closet. "You need this job, it would be better if you went in looking well-kempt rather than a street vagabond."

"You always compare me to a hobo rather than what I intend, which is just someone who is relaxed and comfortable with himself."

"I want you to get this job we need it, we are so behind in bills it will be difficult to catch up before the fall when everything increases in payment from the cold weather."

"I know, I'm not stupid about this you know, I know what to wear and will set a good impression and will get the job so don't be so snide about me."

"I know how you are, you go in with an attitude and tell them too much so they get the wrong impression of you that's why you have no job now or don't keep them very long."

"You're wrong; you know what this city is like, you've been telling me this for years and before we even moved here. You seem to think, though, that it only applies to me. You are the accept ion and everyone is so ready to hire you."

"I've held onto my jobs for six years and longer, you get fired after three months, so I'm telling you to lighten up and be less aggressive, tone it down and say as little as possible. Don't give them your life's story."

"I don't but they ask questions that don't apply to the job and I give them my answers blunt and to the point, maybe that's what they don't like, I don't know. Any way Monday 1:30."

"Right on, I can give you a ride, being that I have the day off if you want?"

"Ya, sure, that would make getting there easier but no arguing or bullshit I'm not interested in going there frustrated or angry."

"Do you want the ride or not?"

"Ya."

The weekend was filled with light-heartedness and BBQ's as they both looked forward to Brent's interview. Monday came and Celina was so excited she had to point out all of Brent's faults of what not to do during the interview and make sure he wore exactly what she had set out for him. This made Brent frustrated and anxious, but he persevered and remained as cool as possible so as not to start arguing over her behaviour.

As they pulled up to the building, they saw that it was a creamery and starring at each other didn't know what the position would be. "Good luck," she said as he got out of the car.

"Thanks!"

Waiting in the lobby for the interview he noticed several different kinds of ice creams and realised it was an ice cream factory. The front office was filled with a variety of cones and ice cream flavours as well as a menu.

"Are you Brent?" the front desk person asked.

"Yes."

"Have a seat and I'll let Sheryl know you're here."

"Okay."

When she returned, she said it would only be a few moments and she'd be right out. He waited there for nearly half an hour wondering what was going on and why it was taking so long. All he could think of was how Celina was going to react as he got back in the car.

Sheryl came out to greet him and brought him to her office. "Have a seat," she said, "and make yourself comfortable."

"Okay," sitting down he found himself observing what was on the table and didn't see anything out of the ordinary. She sat down and he saw that he had a grin that could be taken in two meanings, one that he wasn't what she was expecting or two, he is what she expected but not right for the position.

"I've been going over your resume and I see you from the west coast, what brought you to this province." She asked.

"Well, my wife has family there and she wanted to get reacquainted with them and moving here would be the best way for her to get closer and re-establish relations with them. So we moved here."

"I see you have food-safe, just to be clear, that's why I brought you in for an interview."

"Oh!"

"Also see you have worked as president of a non-profit organisation, what did that entail and why did it end?"

"What we were trying to do is show the abilities of people with disabilities and hopefully find them employable. It did work for a period of time but as the reception set in it was not practical because there were so many people unemployed that they had no consideration to employment. So it was decided by the board of directors to end the society and pursue other prospects. I went into construction for a time and then we decided to move here."

"Oh, and how are you finding it?"

"Different," Brent replied.

"Different? In what way?"

"Well, the people are more aggressive and set a pace of expectation rather than acceptance so I really don't get involved with too many people or circumstances that can lead to problems or heavy socialisation it keeps me more direct and in pursuit of jobs and family."

"Good to hear. We are looking for someone who is flexible with shifts and work in the production of our butter department does this sound like something you would like to try?"

"Yes, sure, I would be interested in anything right now and am open minded to all possibilities."

"Great, we would like someone who could start tomorrow or Wednesday, can you; I mean start on either of these days?"

"Well, I would rather start tomorrow it fits better with my need to be working."

"Great then after I check your references, I'll let you know when you can start."

"Okay, I'll look forward to hearing from you."

That afternoon Brent did hear from Sheryl to start work Wednesday. They were both so excited they went out to their favourite place to eat and ordered their favourite dishes, spending over one hundred fifty dollars.

Chapter 3
The Story

Showing up on the first day Brent was given a tour of the facility and then set with a password as well an FOB to get him in every day. He was then introduced to his supervisor, Cliff, who began introducing him to his role as a part of the printer and wrapper.

"Hey, Brent."

"Hi!"

"This is the printer, that's what we call this whole machine, so there is no confusion where you are. Get it."

"Ya, I guess."

"I'm just about to change the wrap so let me show you how it's done."

"Okay, great."

The rest of the day was filled putting boxes together and building products on pallets. As the day ended Cliff asked, "So, how do you like it?"

"It's production, just like the fish industry. So it's fine," Brent replied.

Leslie, upon seeing Brent, was taken by him immediately, this was his greatest moment. To be in the presence of his next scheme, Brent, a somewhat mild-mannered individual, thought nothing of this place and wanted to make the best of it. He had been looking, for a long time, to fit himself into a position that he could grow with. This s was the opportunity he felt he could work with and make a future for himself, but Leslie had other plans for this person. How he put it was. "My muse has entered the building."

The next day was a little harder, mostly because it was longer, also because the time dragged. While working at the printer, the pusher is a part of the production line and does the boxing. On this day, Brent's second, he met Winston and he was quite the safety manual. Everything stemmed around protecting yourself from being hurt, especially with the pusher.

"This machine can be very dangerous it has a fast base that pushes the butter into position and is very fast. Don't use your right hand but your left, always, when using your right you have to twist it and this can lead to a problem with speed." He showed Brent what he meant, by using each hand to help push the butter into place, that way Brent got a visual of how it should be done and why he shouldn't do it any other way.

As the day continued Brent had a few problems with the butter, at one point the bricks would turn sideways and be crushed in the pusher. Leslie is good at causing this problem, all he has to do is move the guides a fraction and the butter is sent in sideways jamming the pusher and creating a major mess. That's when the whole machine has to be shut down and cleaned. There were a couple of times when the butter would double up and again be crushed and the machine again had to be cleaned.

While Brent was being observed by Winston, Winston saw Brent using his right hand on the pusher and again warned him but included a happening with the person Brent is replacing.

"Brent, I've been watching you and I've seen you using your right hand a couple of times and you've come close with the pusher so I would like to tell you about Steve. Steve was great at his job but that was overtime. When he first started, he was a fumble finger and did things sort of awkwardly. I told him several times, as I am telling you, that he needed to be careful with this machine, but he didn't listen and did things the way he felt comfortable, which was the wrong way.

Well, he continued this for the next few months until it happened. "Winston, looking at the machine began his story."

We were having trouble with the pusher all day and Steve was getting frustrated, after an incident with the butter, he had just finished cleaning the pusher and wanted to complete a box of fifty before turning off the wrapper. He didn't think before doing it, but, using his right hand, pushed the butter into position to complete the box on the machine. All we heard was the scream.

When we looked, he was holding his right hand with his left, in front of his eyes, and the end of his finger, from the knuckle, dangling on a thin string of skin. He was quickly brought to the hospital, and because it was a clean-cut, it was sewed back onto his finger. The same thing happened to another dude, Vince, who up losing his whole arm. "Winston then gave a look of a blank stare at the butter boat and then went onto say, "After it had happened and we were ready to go back to work we had to turn everything back on again and that's when we heard it. It came from the compressor down in the basement. It started out as the sound of it beginning to work but then it went into a huffing and puffing. Cliff and I looked at each other and said, at the same time, "does that sound like laughing to you?"

We stood and listened staring, and simultaneously said, "Vince," and in a matter of concern, we turned it off and started it again with the same results. It took at least five times before it started to sound normal. The day went on without problems but there was an air of strangeness that we couldn't explain we all felt it though. The next day, things were back to normal.

Winston stared off again and then went onto say, "Steve returned to work, after a few weeks off, and everything was okay but, a few months later, it seemed he had more complications. Some form of bacteria had formed in his finger and gangrene had set in so he had to have his whole finger removed." just like Vince but not as serious.

Winston went quiet and the rest of the day, at work, was spent in silence.

Chapter 4

Sherryl, the creamery manager, is a soft-spoken and indiscriminate individual. She is very personable with the employees walking the creamery and checking in on how things are going as well as giving recent orders to be filled through the day or week and employee shift time, when the shift manager is not available or on vacation, but has an underlying personality that is rarely shown yet exposes itself in difficult or troubling circumstances.

To give example; it was after a long weekend, a driver by the name of Toni, had two deliveries in the same location but two different buildings, both had the same address but reversed and adjacent to each other. Toni, a blonde attractive woman, made the deliveries in a timely fashion but got the drops wrong. She was confused by the addresses, being the same numbers and the same street but one was on the northeast and the other was on the northwest.

When Toni got back from the deliveries, at the end of the day, Sherryl unloaded on her, "Are you dyslexic?" she began. "These streets are clearly marked. How could you have screwed up so bad? Now, you have to go back and correct this, and I want it to be done today. This is not the first time for something like this but it is going to be the last. When you get back clean out your locker and don't come in tomorrow."

Toni was history, In contrast to that, Grant, when he was first hired, had some disastrous accidents. On his first week, he was to retrieve some ice cream mix from the freezer that was on the top of the storage wrack, not being used to handling things high on shelving, Grant lost control of the pallet and dropped ten-thousand-dollar worth of product. He was not reprimanded for this or threatened to be fired but given leave for the day as his reasoning was illness and poor judgement because it was affecting his sight.

"That's okay," Sherryl said to Grant go home and come back tomorrow if you're feeling better at that time, if not take tomorrow off as well, "and he did. Now what brings to question is, how is this acceptable? Sherryl was a known lesbian, by most or all the employees, and one would think that she would have a stronger understanding of a female employee than a male.

For the past five years Sherryl and Sam have been spending a lot of personal time together, but because everyone knew Sherryl's sexuality nothing was thought of in their relationship. However, when Toni was fired over a little mistake, that was easily corrected, the staff began to suspect that something was amiss between them.

"Sherryl," Sam, standing at her office door, "can you come to my office in a few when you're done with what you're working on."

"Sure," looking at him inquisitively. After an hour of being engrossed with the next week's schedule, she got up and went to Sam's door and asked, "What's up?"

"Come in and close the door, please," he gestured for her to sit. She closed the door and sat down, not at the chair at his desk but in one at the corner of the bookshelf.

"Okay, so what have you got in mind then?" she questioned.

"Well, I have been scouting and found an interesting subject and would like you to make yourself available for this interaction," he made it very clear that it was not a question of decision but an obligation. "You are involved with me in this whether you want to be or not," looking straight at her, he continued, "This can go very smooth and I need you, "She just sat there staring at him with an ominous grin. "How do you expect this to go down and what time should we meet?"

"We'll meet here around ten, and then set off to the place he resides; the room in the basement has been prepared and be ready to spend the night with this and possibly a few days for this interview." That's what Sam calls these encounters so if it were overheard, by anyone, it would sound innocent and like a matter of business.

I have been watching these two since the creamery moved in, they are very secretive and it's come to my knowledge that there is something going on that I need to discover. Several times, they have come into the building carrying trunks and burying them in the basement, digging the holes one week before.

Sharyl is the only one who knows what happened to the driver, Tim, and of course, I, the caretaker. Helping him discard the body, in the shallow grave under the creamery, she then helps with the clean-up. This takes very little time, everything is on polly and wrapped the blood is drained into a sewage grate outside the container so it goes directly into the city waste, undetectable and clean.

Chapter 5
Chad

The morning was blustery and thickly draped with smoke from the forest fires coming from the province that bordered this one. As Brent began making his morning coffee, he turned on the weather channel to see what the day was going to throw at him. It turned out to be scheduled for clear skies but during the night, when he got up to have a cigarette, he saw that the moon had a reddish tint to it. Not a good sign.

The fires in the mountains were so severe that work agencies throughout the province were being asked to send teams of workers to battle them. Brent, before getting this latest employment, was deciding whether he should join and be a part of this programme. He had been out of steady work for going on three years and it would have brought in the needed money to turn everything around.

All his bills were two months in arrears and threatened to be cut off. Having to be at work by six, Brent would get up at three to make coffee and begin the preparation of the day's agenda.

Stepping outside to catch the bus at 4:50, he could smell the hint of smoke in the air and thought to himself, "the *fires must be huge to have this smell all over the city."*

As he walked to the bus stop, he wondered what it would be like to have been involved in battling fires like that. His long-time girlfriend, after mentioning that he was going to sign up, did not want him to get involved with that kind of work fearing for his safety.

"It's good money, and it will pull us out of the arrears we have accumulated these past few months."

"No," she said abruptly. "You are prone to accidents and you would be mixed with all types of individuals and you tend to instigate aggressive behaviour. That is not good, you would end up pissing someone off and getting yourself hurt bad or dead."

"How optimistic of you!"

Stepping off the bus to start his three-minute walk to the building he bumped into Chad. Chad is the typical employee who takes on all the labouring positions that need to be done before the operators start with the daily workload. He would set pallets of butter into place to be pushed into the butter boat, transfer pallets of salt to the churns, help with labelling boxes for the yoghurt milk and set bricks of butter for the person working with the buttercups.

Buttercups are little one spread serving for toast in cafés or restaurants and only one person needed to be on that machine but there are times when there would be two operating it for a more effective workload. He would also be a part of the boxing of whipped butter in a 454 g containers. His conversation, no matter what the subject, would always lead to the topic of drugs.

"Hey!"

"How's it goin', Brent?"

"I don't know. I won't know until I get into seeing what I'm in for today."

"Ya, I hear that."

Chad would find himself wandering the corridors looking for things to do when he had finished a task, such as labelling or setting butter bricks. "*I, the caretaker, have been watching this go on since he started. An intolerant individual who likes to hear his own voice and believes his opinion is the only thing for others to consider, not letting anyone give their idea a voice and interjecting observation and critique jest as he enters a room without listening or understanding what's being discussed.*"

Following him while he wonders, looking for something to do, the caretaker often instructs Leslie to disturb him by tripping him up or putting an obstacle in his way. Sometimes Leslie will mix up the stickers and Chad, always in his own thoughts, would often find himself redoing the bottles or jugs he had stared, with the proper labels. It would go unnoticed but he becomes frustrated and gets louder in conversation. This makes Leslie very excited and, wanting to continue his interference, brings out many ideas to disturb Chad's daily agenda.

Leslie loved making problems in the production area because it involved three different areas, the Ice cream room, the cups and patties as well as solids, which he did a great trick on Brent a few times, he had great fun with Brent. His favourite, though, is the butter area it provided many different ideas for disturbance and intrigue.

To give an example; Chad, whenever he works in that area, will be the focus of Leslie's attention. This one time he was working in the boxing area carrying packed boxes to the pallet and whenever Leslie felt like he would put extra weight on the box causing Chad to drop the box. These were open boxes and it would cause a major mess that not only had to be cleaned but the butter could not be re-boxed and it would either go into rework, which means back to pasteurisation or into the second stage butter boat. The second stage butter boat is where butter is thrown when the registry is out or the wrap is not set right as well if the butter weight is wrong, which is a regular happening, especially during setup.

Leslie also loved to mess with behaviour and conflicting personalities, that's why he had a major interest in Brent. Like this night, Brent was again on his own, with Stan as the churn operator, and Leslie, with his soaring excitedness, was too ready to fuck his night up, and he did.

It started slowly, with the registry, it was a change of wrap and with it comes the setting up of the paper to be centralised to the folds. What Leslie would do is, by touching the paper in a certain place, while being fed into the wrapping machine, it would skew the registry. He did this continuously for the first hour and then got bored; because Brent didn't give the right response.

Moving on he began to cause ripping and sending unwrapped butter to the belt. Brent showed a little more frustration with this, pleasing Leslie, but it still wasn't enough. This, though, went on for at least three major cleans.

Pleased with himself Leslie decided to make the night more interesting and began focusing on the pusher as well.

Chapter 6

The owner Sam was a large burly man with an easy temperament, he overlooked people for their mistakes knowing that things happened, especially when rushed or in highly stressful situations. Sam had a casual sense of his office leaving a space open to any new ideas to expand or find the resource, offering no explanation for things he might do at random. He liked to walk the different areas and mingle with the employees to get a feel of how they were and know whether they were content with their jobs and the way things were.

Every year, he held elaborate Christmas parties that were filled with gifts and exotic foods. He offered great travel packages for his sales team and a great medical plan and RSP for all employees. This kept long-term employment, with the people who liked the job and chose to maintain their employment with the company.

As a traditionalist, he liked to maintain old standards and uses traditional machinery to make his products such as ice cream, butter and yoghurts to name a few. This however kept the maintenance crew always busy and in a stressful position of repair. Outdated machines make it hard to find replacement parts and machining them is sometimes the only way to maintain them.

Sam was a reader as well he read on many different writing interests but the one, he read most was of serial killers and crime. He brought his reading to the office and made no effort to hide his reading; he also had books on time travel and psychology. Physics was also a great interest, reading books on Albert Einstein, Nostradamus and other not well-known publications.

He and Sherryl had an unusually close business relationship, but everyone in the office thought nothing of it being that their temperaments seemed to be similar as well their involvement with the way things were run, mixing with the staff as well as giving support to people in need of extra attention.

On one particular day, a trucking accident right outside the creamery. A driver had not been observant of the signage before leaving the yard and took a righthand turn, where he should not have. He hit a guarded fire hydrant and pulled it from its base, resulting in a twenty-five-thousand-dollar municipal charge for the fixing of this avoidable situation.

Being a new employee and knowing this would not sit well with the owner, Sam, the driver immediately quit. Sam called him into the office the next day, everyone was surprised to see him in, but Sam wanted to give him a long haul across the border as he was the only one with the certification to do a haul like that and was why he was hired in the first place. He accepted the job and took the truck on the road, so when he didn't return and a week later saw the truck in the yard there was nothing suspect other than he didn't work at the creamery anymore."

What was observed by the caretaker was that Sam had met with the driver after loading, with a different driver assumed from a temp agency, and replaced the driver with a temp. Sam then took the drive, Tim, out for a meal just to break the tension. When they returned Sam was holding Tim up, arms draped over each other's shoulders, as Sam took him into his office.

"I can't have the kind of behaviour you have displayed in my company; it must be treated as you have treated me, with aggression and hostility. You have attacked my domain and sent it into a spiral that cannot be stopped without retribution," Sam went into an insane sense of self and Tim couldn't make out what he was saying, but he knew it wasn't good before he passed out all he saw was Sam going into a box and searching.

Upon waking up Tim discovered that he had been tied to a chair, his shirt was off and his bare feet were in a bowl of water and he had only shorts on.

"Well, Tim," Sam said curtly. "It looks like your time is at an enduring end, what I have in mind is to put these two electro patches on you and find out how high I can make you jump, without leaving the floor of course, but I also have a secondary pleasure that you will enjoy."

Sam always transfers the pleasure of his acts to the victim he makes the idea he is introducing one of distance to himself and of direct euphoria to his subject, "BY placing an electro pad on either side of your temples and two on the back of your neck and then another two around the lower part of your calves, I make sure that the charge is throughout your entire body. This gives me a complete area of mass to play with, when there is an electrical charge going through you, feeling pain is eliminated. So let's give you a little trickle to find out where your temperament is."

He pulled out a small electrical box, one that would be used to charge an electric train set, "These boxes are very practical." Sam smiled. "They have a charge that sends the right message, for instance."

Hooking up the electro lines from Tim to the power box, Sam continued to explain, "I have three boxes to hook you up to, so, I can do them all at once or one at a time but to get the maximum effect three charges are needed."

Sam then went to a knife wrack, where some very intimidating knives were hung, "With these, I create a masterpiece," showing Tim his collection, there were several sizes of butcher knives along with some very long slicing knives, deboning knives as well and thinner knives for probing or just small cuts and poking.

Sam doesn't like noise, yelling, screaming, loud chatter, intense conversation or arguing. The way he has set the pads on his victim makes a perfect pain drain, and like a surgeon, he can do his wielding in silent reproach. Sam enjoys the sacrifice of men; they have a bitter sense of it and are always ready to fight right into the final stages.

Women, though, always breakdown to tears, no matter how tough they start out, they begin a trail of tears with the history of their lives pains and disasters and, while pleading for their lives, they always resort to sex as a way to satisfy and be able to go home. With Sam, it's not about sex; it's about life longevity. Females are weak and their meat and hearts are always flawed. The meat from a woman is not firm it is like a jell, it has nobody, and he found that no matter how hard or how much they work out once the meat leaves the bone it has the same consistency.

A man, on the other hand, as long as they are without compromise, like drug or alcohol abuse, or small in size, and Tim is healthy has a better meat density and sinewy. Sam, though, over the years has had to make some expected compromises, because of the growing drug use, he has taken that into account and use and abuse are two different animals and use is acceptable.

Sam knows that it isn't the quantity of what's taken but the quality of it, starting at the calves he takes out a small blade, turns on the box and starts poking Tim, to find out what he is feeling, all Tim did was stare. Staring back at him Sam took his first piece, but then remembered, "My kitchen," he said aloud.

Pulling out the hot burner and some spice, he took a marble cutting board and placed the piece of calving on it. Tim didn't even feel it cut from him but saw that it was significant, "What the fuck did you just do?" he emphasised. The charge was going through his legs and that's all he could feel. Tim watched as Sam spiced up the meat and let it sit, turning on the burner of the hot plate, low heat to cook slowly.

Sam then grabbed a bigger knife and stood over Tim, "I have been watching you and the way your body has been moving, and I like what I see from the right; your left thigh was the first intrigue, but it's your right thigh that has a certain response I like."

Sam turned to the boxes and turned on the two electrodes on the back of Tim's neck, feeling the serge, Tim could only sit and shake when Sam, holding the long slim knife took it and cut an inch of thigh off Tim, from the groin to his knee, "Ahhhhhhhhhhh…" is all that Tim could let out.

And Sam placing it on the marble, took the piece, spiced in garlic and season salt with a dab of BBQ spice, his own preparation, one he got from a cookbook, and placed it on the heated pan after adding oil and butter on it.

Smiling he said aloud, "Smell that aroma," and began spicing the other piece, taken from Tim's thigh.

Turning the piece on the pan he looks over at Tim and smiling, "I like it when the skin gets crispy."

Tim just sat staring at Sam shaking from the current going through him. Sam, satisfied by the cooked piece, began to eat it, taking out a bottle of BBQ sauce, hickory, "Everything tastes better with hickory, wouldn't you agree."

Tim just stared.

After finishing the piece, he pulled out a bottle of red merlot and poured it into a crystal wine glass. Taking a sip, he then put the thigh onto the pan, after adding butter. Then grabbing the long thin knife, Sam turned and looked at Tim again wondering what he wanted next. Tim has a big abdomen, and Sam knew that it would be all fat, not a good choice, but Tim's arms are all muscle, and he liked that.

"*Just the choice cuts*," he thought to himself and then said it aloud to Tim, "Just, the choice cuts," and he cut the inside left arm, from the armpit to the elbow.

Tim's arms were tied so all he could do is again watch and scream, "Ahhhhhhhh…" surprising, but the electrodes help with this as well; there is very little blood.

Putting the piece on the marble cutting board, "You can scream all you want, but in this transporting can, it has been noise proofed and tested on one will hear you," Sam gloated while spicing the newly extracted piece.

Tim, staring tried to get out a word, "I'm going to kill you," he said shaking and stuttering in electric current.

Sam smiled and turned to his knives and grabbed one of the large chopping knives and turned on the temple electrodes, "This is the final," he said aloud and with a swift chop to the left side of Tim's chest. Breaking the upper ribs with the blade, he pulled it free and proceeded to chop the right side, which inflicted the same deep gash. This time, the blood was oozing down to the floor onto the plastic polly Sam had placed under the chair, to make cleaning a lot easier.

These blows were the final phase of Sam's need and Tim's last visual; he was dead in a few seconds. Then Sam pulled out a bone cutter and cut through Tim's chest, pulling off the bone mass; he extracted the heart with the thinner blade and cut it in half, putting one-half in Tim's lap and the other on the marble board.

The piece on the burner was ready, and he took it off and placed it on a large serving plate. Sam began spicing the arm piece and the half heart and, after adding more butter placed them both on the pan, "this is one employee I will remember," he said aloud, as he began pouring another glass of wine and took out some pickles and Havarti as well as gouda to add to the delicacy of his meal.

Chapter 7
Leslie

It was a clear night and Leslie was just finishing his last run for the day and would be back at the creamery in a few hours. Pulling into the loading bay, he began to feel a sharp pain down his left arm. While he was unloading the last skid he slammed into a skid of boxes with a loaded pallet on the pallet jack, he hit it hard, and the pain shot through his left side right to his toes.

"Fucking shit, I fucking knew it was there, how could I have done that," he said aloud, knowing he was the only one on the loading dock. It took a few moments to regain his composure and when he did, though he still felt the pain in his arm, he knew during the drive back it would probably disappear.

On the drive back to the creamery, the pain did not go away and he started to also get a headache so he pulled to the shoulder and stopped to take four Ibuprofens, hopeful that would relieve some of the pain and the headache. The drive was at least two hours, after backing into the loading bay; he then went to his own truck and, after starting it, pulled it around beside the delivery truck he had just parked.

There was still enough room for him to back into the docking bay and do what he needed to do. Going into the building, and entering the cooler, he saw that the skid he had set aside, for his own sale, before leaving on his last drop, was still there. It was a small stack of the product he had left behind, his last drop was a full load and this one didn't fit into the cube. So he made sure it was mixed with the next day's orders and would not be noticed.

Leslie had been taking the product in this manner for a few years now and it had always gone unnoticed, tonight was no different, and the extra money it gave him made the difference of what he felt he was owed after working here all these years and not given any satisfaction for his time or acknowledgement for his long hours of work. Walking to retrieve the pallet jack he felt the pain in his arm subside and was relieved that it wouldn't be an issue as he loaded his truck.

He slipped the pallet jack under the skid and lifted it. As he began to pull it a massive pain pierced his head and down his left side, slipping and falling on the spot, he hit the floor hard as he fell backwards and smashed his head fracturing his skull on the concrete. Standing there, staring at himself, Leslie began mumbling, "What the fuck?" he questioned, "Is that me? How?" And that's how I, the caretaker, found him.

When the shipping crew began to arrive, they found Leslie lying on the floor, "What the fuck," Karen said allowed, "How long has he been here like this? Call the EMS. I think we should close for the day while this is investigated."

That's when Sherryl walked in, hearing what Karen was saying, and agreed, "Yes, we need to bring in the police and the coroner. It looks like he's had a heart attack. I think it's safe to say that this is of natural causes rather than something suspicious or criminal."

She said looking at the shipping staff. When the police arrived Sherryl was the one to greet them and began explaining the situation, "Leslie was discovered this morning when the shipping crew began showing up at 4:30," Sherryl explained. "We believe he was starting to reload his truck when it happened, but we are unsure."

They closed the Creamery, for the day, while the police did a minor investigation. It was determined, by the EMS paramedics, that he had suffered a massive heart attack and he was dead before he hit the floor.

That is how the caretaker found him, standing over himself staring, and mumbling," What the fuck, is that me? How? What am I to tell my family?" over and over, for at least an hour or two, the time has no meaning in this way two hours could pass as two days and nothing changes, except with what we make happen. The caretaker brought Leslie to the chicken coup and began to explain to him what he is now, "You are with me now, my employee; we will be working together to keep this place in order. That being said, we have a responsibility, weeding out the weak-minded."

Chapter 8

The night crew consists of three employees, unsupervised; they are expected to have at least ten skids, minimum, completed nightly. At this time, there is Tom, Stan and Austin, on the night crew. Tom is conflicted with responsibility and doesn't work to complete the night's tasks but takes account of all that he's done and numbers it off like an agenda of who's done what and separates each chore into numbers of comparison to accomplished duty.

Now Stan, in his elder years, continues to work, but wants no part in conflict just that the tasks of the night's responsibilities are being done. His physical ability is limited to what he does with the churning of the butter and even the butter tray, for transporting the butter to the butter boat, is difficult and he relies on Austin to help.

Austin is a capable middle-aged man who has worked for other companies, in the same field, knows his responsibilities for the job. He just has trouble with wrapping paper changes and relies on Tom who has just as much trouble or more because of his lack of focus due to ADHD. Constantly blaming his difficulties on his medications and one day, after he stopped taking them, just disappeared.

Tom's conversations, when not counting down his already accomplished duties, always streamed around not wanting to be doing this forever and maybe moving onto churning or disappearing to live elsewhere like Germany or Mexico. He smoked a lot of pot and didn't care to be discreet, smoking it in front of the building's exterior security cameras. The owner, Sam, would often be watching and saw what was going on with Tom, also hearing the complaints from Austin, wanted him replaced but couldn't find the right person to fit the position.

During one evening after changing the wrapping paper successfully, one week before being dismissed, "I really do like this job," he exclaimed to Austin. Austin just stood there looking at him for a moment wondering when his next outburst was going to happen, It was usually after a misshape with the pusher or the belt, sometimes the butter would turn to the side and be smooshed in the pusher and the whole machine would then be shut down while he cleaned the pusher.

Just then that's when Austin heard it, "Fuuuuuuuuuuuuuck, this fucking machine," a loud outcry came from behind the pusher, not only was there a twisted mess in the pusher, but the wrapping paper had also skewed and messed up and there was butter everywhere.

This kind of happening often took at least thirty to forty-five minutes to clean but because Tom has no patience with this continuous happening, he freaks out, and instead, it would take two and a half hours.

"I'm going out for a smoke" and left. They both knew what to expect. When he returned, he had a big grin and went to work cleaning both sides of the machine. It took him one hour and forty-five minutes; they both left him to do it because if they tried to help, he would take it as dysfunction as if Tom didn't know what he was doing.

As he, Tom, began the ritual of setting up the wrapping machine, starting it up, everything went normal but he forgot one step and the wrap registry was out. These are the moments that I wait for, I can enter a body in these seconds of frustration and anger, and I crossed into him at the time of the next happening.

Leslie touched the wrapping paper, and when Tom started up the machine, it went well for a few minutes, but then again, the wrap skewed to the right, "Fuuuuuuck!" is all Stan and Austin heard.

And Tom was back cleaning and resetting the wrapper. "You fucking machine you better work for me now or I'm going to smash the shit out of you," Tom screamed. Austin, concerned, went over.

"Is everything okay?" he asked.

"YES!" he yelled back, taking it as a slight against his knowledge of the machine and ability.

Austin went back to pushing blocks of butter. Both he and Stan stared at each other for a moment, then at Tom and then went back to what they were doing.

From that moment, Tom must have got it right; everything went well through the rest of the night. Tom was in a pretty good mindset thinking he had done a good job that night so Stan took the opportunity to give him the news, "Tom," Stan motioned him to come over, "I'm out of here, and you two should be finished in an hour and a half, by 11:30? Right?" he asked.

"Ya, I guess if everything goes well," Tom implied.

"Great, I am also to let you know that next week is your final week here and you'll be dismissed before the next cut off."

"Oh." Tom looked at Stan then at the floor pouting.

"Are you going to be, okay?" Stan asked.

"Oh, ya don't worry about it," he said confidently.

"Okay," Stan went to his car and left. The night was quiet for the rest of the shift.

"So, what did Stan say to you before he left?" Austin enquired.

"Oh, he just told me this is my last week here."

"Oh, are you okay with that?"

"Ya, I was going to quit anyway?"

"That's not what you implied earlier tonight."

"I know but that was just wishful thinking."

After doing the nightly clean up, Tom went through his agenda count down, to do as little as possible, which Austin really, really hated. They got ready to punch out and leave.

Tonight, Tom was driving so he offered to drive Austin to the c-train, and he accepted. The drive was a quiet one, neither of them spoke, and Tom knowing where to drop Austin took him to the LRT station.

When they arrived at the station Tom mentioned that he wasn't going straight home but dropping off the car, at his Mom's, and getting on the bus to be at home later than planned. Austin sat wondering why he even mentioned it and got out of the car to catch his train.

"Thanks, and I'll see you Monday night."

"Ya, right," he said and drove off.

Dropping off the car to his Mom's he, instead of going in, just put the keys in the mailbox, then headed to the bus stop. As he boarded the red line he came up with an idea. The caretaker actually created the notion of this indignant plan. Getting off at 39th avenue LRT station he walked down 25th towards the creamery.

It took him thirty-five minutes and, using his FOB, entered the creamery building. He went into the change room and took off his clothes, putting them into the laundry cabinet, knowing no one would see them there.

Now naked, he began walking around the plant and walked into the pasteurising area, crawled into a silo, and skulked in behind the agitation fan. It was the most hidden spot, and if no one looked, he would not be seen. Squatting in a spot behind the agitator, he, using the edge of the blade to rest his head on, fell into a deep sleep.

That morning, Nate arrived early with the expectation of delivery of cream. He turned on the agitator without looking in first, just to test it, not knowing that Tom was sleeping with his head on the blade. The blade of the fan spun and cut through Tom's neck so deep it severed his curated artery instantly. He bled out in two minutes.

After Tom expired, the caretaker could not continue to possess him and had to re-join Leslie. Nate, still not looking into the silo, shut the door and began draining the cream from the truck into the silo, covering Tom.

Tom's body had gone limp and with the cream, filling around him, his body slipped flat out onto the bottom of the silo, then, turning on the agitator; the blood, from Tom, was mixed with the cream. There was enough cream in the silo that the mixture went unnoticed, and after pasteurisation, the plasma would be thoroughly mixed with the cream and would not compromise the cream's composition or be detected.

This went on, without the discovery of Tom was in the silo, for three silo fills and with each cream dump Tom became more and more distilled. On the weekend, due to no cream, had been shut down. Through the weekend, Tom began to ferment, when it opened again Monday someone noticed an odour coming from one of the silo's and, after looking into each one on, found Tom's body. No one could figure out how long he had been there and thought it to have happened on the Friday before the weekend and with, only, the one day's production.

After the discovery of Tom, the creamery closed during the investigation and inspection of the silo and through the week closed until every silo was cleaned and sterilised. The two churns also went through thorough sterilisation as well. There was dumping of all the butter produced that Friday to ensure it did not get onto the retail shelves of stores, but, I, the caretaker, no different.

There were three different fillings and the first one was the one that really counted, because of the mixing of the blood, with the cream, it had produced butter for three different orders that night and went out the next day's deliveries. The same went with the next fill; it wasn't until the third fill of cream, in the silo, that Tom was discovered. That butter, produced by this cream, was not going out until Monday, so it was sitting in the freezer waiting to be loaded onto trucks and delivered.

Chapter 9
The Auger

It was a dark dismal day the clouds had hung over the city and put a chill into the bones of everyone who challenged getting out that morning. The threat of snow was in the air and gave the people something to talk about on their travels to work.

Nate's shit started at 3:30, he had been switched to nights because Stan had taken two weeks holidays and Nate was the person, being new and showing a genius to operate several departments, pasteurisation, mixing, as well as the churn, was taking over for the next two weeks in Stan's place. Nate did not like working these long nights and made it clear at the beginning of the shift.

The night started off normal everything went, as usual, Nate, conversed with the dayshift operator and talked about what was in the churn at this time. He came in just as the salt was to be added and mixed into the butter. The afternoon crew would be arriving in an hour and the second churn would be ready for them to wrap. That was the change to unsalted, which was the conversation he had before relieving the day shift blender.

"Hey Craig, what's up?" Nate questioned.

"I'm just getting ready to put the salt in then I'm out of here."

"Great I'll take it from there you just bolt I know you want to go out for dinner with your family so just take off I'll look after this."

"Right on, flex." That was the nickname given Nate after showing a genius to the workings of the production.

"Have a great time and say hi to your wife for me."

"Ya, sure."

After adding the salt and making small preparations for Nate, he shot out of the room and palmed out. That was the name given to the clock used when starting a shift. It was a new device that reads your palm signature to verify you had shown up.

Nate stared at the door and watched him leave then leaned back against the wall to observe what the butter in the churn was doing. This is the shift change, and waiting for the cream to break in one churn and the mixing of salt in the other takes time and observation. Nate, during this time, would find himself alone and would lean up against the wall contemplating his studies and anticipating when he would be in his element of working for himself as an electrician.

During the nights at work, he would bring in the text to read or quizzes to go through just to test himself, while waiting for the cream to break or blending the salt, everything takes time and different creams, depending on the percentage of fats have different yields and longer breaking duration. This cream, they were using tonight, was a low percentage, about twenty-eight per cent fat and took forty-five minutes, to an hour, to break.

During this time, the wrapping crew would wonder and find other things to do or take their breaks. But this is a shift change and the day crew left to the lunchroom, and wait for the salted churn to be ready for wrapping. They would usually take their last break at that time to make the final part of the day go faster. The evening crew, after all, would be arriving in an hour.

So Nate finding himself alone decided to do some reading. When the butter had been mixed for the right period of time, he stopped the churn and opening the Plexiglas door he thought to himself, "*Must get a sample for the lab, this is the most innocuous part of the job. I should spit on it just to give the lab something to think about or act on.*"

Then he started to laugh and caught it before it became boisterous. "I should sperm this one just to see what the reaction would be from the lab," he thought in a wicked moment of absurdity. Taking the sample and walking it to the lab he had this foolish grin and couldn't help continuing to chuckle to himself. He then checked the moisture, and everything was good, 17.5.

Getting back to the churn, he observed that he was still alone and proceeded to move the butter to the boat, that was the name given to the auger, but first he needed to turn it on and did so. He grabbed the butter table to move it to the churn and begin transporting the mix to the auger.

As he pulled the first load from the churn, he thought to himself, "This feels a little heavier than usual."

It seemed odd and had a little trouble pulling it from its port. Clumsily, he rolled it around the churns, of which there were, two, and pulled the table around to the auger.

As he was in the motion of setting it, he noticed a brick of butter on the floor and thought, "Fucking wrapper operators are so sloppy; they can't even pick up a brick to keep the way clear for me."

Previously the shift before, an unknown to him had turned up the auger because of high moisture in the load before this and didn't inform him or turn it down during the shift change. Nate, while stepping over the fallen brick of butter, to avoid slipping took a bigger step than usual but failed to see there was a second clump just where his foot hit the floor and slipped.

Falling, his hands slippery from handling the butter, he let go of the table that, because he liked to fill it to the max, was heavier than normal and it slammed into his chest. His arms, flailing to the ceiling, had nothing to grab to prevent him from landing head first into the auger. As he fell backwards into the boat his head hit the blades and the force of the blow sliced through his skull and into his brain deep enough to wedge him tight on the auger blades. This started a series of actions that he could not avoid or prevent.

One, the counter circular motion made it impossible to pull himself off or up, the blades were turning into each other. Two, instead of being able to wrap his leg around the butter table he ended up pushing it away. Three, the auger in its counteraction began pulling his head into the bottom of the boat and strangled him so he couldn't yell for help. Four, as the auger began pulling his body into the boat and slicing deeper into his head the augers also began to crush his chest, slicing into his spine and torso cutting his organs into a ground mush, against the bottom of the butter boat. Five, his arms and legs were twisted and contorted so heavily that there was nothing more he could do but die.

When the wrapping crew finally arrived, he was still bleeding out into the boat. Horrified finding Nate in this disturbing state, they ran to the lab to call for help, finding no one there so they bolted to the front office and in their excitement could only get out, "He's dead," and pointed in the direction of the production room. "Call 911" and broke down crying.

They all walked to the production area to observe the body.

"Who is it?" asked someone from the ice cream department.

"I think, it's Nate," said Craig.

Just then Nate walked in. "Holy shit, Nate!" They all shouted in unison, and with the same motion, they all looked down at the body in the boat, "Who the fuck is this then?"

"Where's Winston," asked Nate while they were looking at the figure in the boat.

Nate then bent over and reached into the boat, pulled out a pair of glasses and exclaimed, "I think I know who this is, Winston. How could this have happened? He's usually more careful than this, to end up crushed in the auger?

It was me, again taking advantage of the moment. Winston would always be at the boat making sure the butter was properly set in the augers to be fed into the wrapper. That was my moment, he was there alone, and the butter bowl, used for transferring the butter from the churn to the boat, was right behind him.

Opportunity, he bent over to reach into the boat, after dropping his glasses into it, that's when I acted giving the butter tray a push and bumping Winston into the augers. He didn't even scream or make a noise of any kind; it was perfect, but a little disappointing. One would think that even an "oh fuck," would be a response but he said nothing.

Leslie and I both stood over him and watched; it was glorious. We had no idea augers could do such incredible work so fast. Of course, with our combined gifts of manipulation, we sped up the augers to make them a little more effective and quicker.

Chapter 10

During Brent's first two months, he met a guy by the name of Chad. Chad is a heavyset individual with a faults sense of high energy; his drug addiction gives him the ability to do his work, at the creamery, with speed and intensity but drags him around with a loud, attention deficit that annoys other employees with loquacious conversation.

Easily distracted, as someone enters the room, he includes himself in conversation when either not knowing the subject or thinking he has complete knowledge of what is being discussed. When he does this, he overwhelms and takes control not letting anyone get in a word, edgewise, not realising the people had just stopped listening and moved onto another topic. While in discussion, he is not subtle his tone is loud and obnoxious and he takes everyone through the drama of what he thinks should be known.

He does the same in the place he lives, not as an owner, as the person managing the residence, he will see something he would like changed and without consulting the owner begins the project. Then when the owner comes to collect rent, he will give a reason why he had to make the change to the area he has been working on and begin handing receipts to the owner expecting a rent reduction or reimbursement.

Chad brings this conversation to work as well. I was working on the kitchen, to make it more spacious and accessible, and as the owner walked in, surprising me, and with a weird questioning look on his face, I began to tell him why I was doing this. I had already torn out the cupboards, the sink, and the floor tiles, it took me half a day to do it, but I was high on three hits of E and smoking pot the whole time.

Anyway, he, the owner, asked me what the hell I was doing, just like that. So I began to tell him about a leak in the drainage under the sink in the kitchen and the damage it caused to the counter and cabinets.

I then told him about the linoleum and how I discovered that the leak had caused it to curl and bubble so it had to be torn out and replaced then. After tearing out the sink, I noticed that black fungus was growing all up the wall, and so I had to tear out the upper cupboards to tear out the wall so it could be cleaned and changed.

All he did was, staring at me for five minutes, began looking around and said, "I will not reduce your rent any more than it already has or pay for the work, you did this without talking to me about it first, and I will not pay you for the damage you caused, but keep the receipts, and I can reimburse you for the cost of materials."

I told him that I didn't expect to be paid for the work, but it had to be done because of the damage that I saw and the smell. He agreed but then added that the next time, I wanted anything done like this, I was to phone and go over it with him and not just start ripping things apart. I agreed and paid my rent handed him the bills I saved from what I had already bought and he left."

Two trailers were gutted by Chad and Tom, a new employee who knew Chad, and Tom tells the story of where he was living and just by mentioning what he would like having done to two trailers he owned.

The first conversation Brent had with him was working in the whipped butter area putting lids on 250 kg containers.

"Hey!"

"Hey, man." A slight pause and then looked right in my eyes, "Have you ever skydived, man?"

"No."

"You got to go; it's the greatest thing. It's just like flying man. Especially if you're afraid of heights, I am and that's how I challenged it for me, you know?"

"Well, I am afraid of heights, and I challenged it in a different way, rather than jumping out of a plane."

"I was just telling Winston here and I want to take him up to try this, he was telling me about his fear of heights, and I want him to challenge it by doing this. I was on three hits of acid when I did it, and holy shit, it was the biggest rush I ever felt in my life, three hits of acid man!"

"Well, that would have been quite the rush if your parachute didn't open, hey?"

"I was tethered to a jumper who has done this many times, you know?"

"Oh, well, I guess that makes it safer for you then."

"Ya, man. You should go."

"No, what I've got to do now though is go back to the wrapper their dumping and I'm needed there."

Later that week, I met with Chad after work, as we were walking, he told me a thing he had done to the butter while it was being made in the churn.

I've been watching the guy on the churns and he leaves the churn open and unattended while he's adding salt, so, I had this plan. I went out and spent three hundred dollars on liquid acid and took it to work. I waited until Bob had left the churn open.

Doing his thing with the salt, but that day he had left to do something else as well and left it unattended, for at least five minutes, before returning. That's when I took the opportunity to act, the vile was in my pocket, and I strolled by the churn and emptied the whole vile onto the butter.

He began to laugh slightly, "Can you imagine how many people it affected? They wouldn't even know they were high or ripped."

"You realise little kids eat that as well, right?"

"Well, what would it do really? Just give them more energy during the time they were eating it; anyway, that was six months ago. It has to be all sold by now, and there hasn't been anything in the news about it or any major disasters, has there?"

"No, but not all work-related accidents get reported and they don't do blood tests after a situation so how would anyone know?"

"Ya, and that's a good thing, hey?"

"Hmmmmmmmm…you're not planning on doing that again, are you?"

"Na, it was a one-time thing, and I just felt like sharing that day."

Charlie is a loner and works in the mixing department by himself; he doesn't like Chad and lets him know it by calling him a crack head.

One day, while arriving to work, Brent overheard the two of them in conversation.

"Hey, crack head," the greeting Charlie gave him on the rare occasions when they passed each other.

"I told you not to call me that. If you keep saying that to me, you're going to regret it."

"Oh, ya, what do you think you're going to do?"

"Just stop or else."

That was as far as it went, and everyone went back to work, as normal. We were watching, and this is what we like to hear. It gives a way to direct actions for a future encounter. What we do is create little incidents; such as moving objects, this creates an impression of suspense it also lets people know we're here, also tripping up a procedure; for example, Nate, during one of his shifts on the churns, was putting cream into the churns, and each time, we made sure it was an overfill.

In this way, we are now in control of the breaking of the cream; how this works is: after it breaks, it needs to be washed and water added for the moisture levels.

While this was going on, I put more added water than needed; it wasn't accidental. This happens because of the extra cream added, and Nate's thinking that with this happening he needed to add more water for a proper moisture level. This is wrong, because, it was an illusion; by creating a higher level of cream, more moisture would have to be added, but what was really done was this. We can make levels of fluids rise and fall so by shear will, between the both of us; the level of cream appeared higher. More moisture would be needed, and therefore, an overfill was done by Nate.

He freaked, throwing things all over the production room, blaming people for leaving things lying around, complaining about the facility and how rundown it is, "What the fuck, how am I to get things done right when I'm tripping all over things? These shouldn't be here,"

And he kicked the wrenches lying at the side of the churn but in the middle of the floor beside the butter boat. Just then Craig walked in, and Nate left without saying anything.

That was incredible; we both stood back and watched all; Leslie stuck the tools where they ended up but in realistic terms, Nate did it and blamed everyone on shift but himself. His typical behaviour and without a blink or apology, he went home.

Chapter 11
The Lab

Brenda, a very curt personality, although she is heavyset, she has a beautiful look, blonde and confidence shown in the way she expresses herself. She sits at the head of the department of QA (quality assurance) and takes her job very serious leaving no position or department out of her evaluation. Contamination, to her, is something that should never happen and makes sure it never will while she is there.

To prevent this she has a change routine that plays on the whole building: when the change of shifts begins the people from the outside have to step into sterilising liquids, then, shower and change into fresh clothes. They then must sterilise anything going into the packaging department so there is a sterilising micrometre on the door to the supply room as well as the door at the entrance of the wrapping room. Her position also includes taste testing, which is her favourite part of the job and holds taste sittings at least twice weekly. When new flavours are introduced, she puts little cups out for all the employees to try with feedback questionnaires.

I, the caretaker, have a strong disposition for that kind of behaviour it creates unnecessary tension and frustration. I have instructed Leslie to let her know we're watching her so he plays with her in ways she would know that she is being observed by something or someone.

He, while she is walking through the production area, would move the butter table, right in front of her. Now they, because of the unevenness of the floors, would dismiss it as an act of gravity due to the flooring's imperfections. He would also toy with her computer, making it skip data, delete data, as well; he would tap her shoulder or brush past her. This was taken, by her like a wisp of air from the ventilation, Brenda would often mention how weird it was to feel this kind of air movement because it would happen at times when it was turned off or when she wasn't in front of the vents.

We both would find pet peeves, things that put her off for the day and play on that through each week. The production workers wouldn't know why she was upset but just know to stay out of her way while she was there.

Being a tall big-boned girl, her size always intimidated most of the employees. Like on this one occasion, Brenda had come into the production area and, looking for anything to start off with, "Why are these boxes here? Should they not be in the chicken coup?" she questioned, "And these rolls, are there not used rolls of the same wrap by the loading dock? Can you not use them first rather than new?"

"There were issues with those rolls, and they were putting us behind by two almost three churns, so we had to change it because of that, so now we have new rolls; it's running better and we're up to speed."

"I would like to see them used or marked with a note letting supplies know so they can be replaced," she then went onto suggest. "And the pallets of boxes, here in the production room, we have a place for them in the chicken coup why are they not kept there? Remove these, and don't set them there again or someone is going to be written up."

Craig offered his piece with, "They are there to make them more accessible when production is at full pace, that way we aren't running back and forth to the chicken coup it's all right in front of us to be used."

"This is not where they are meant to be and I don't want to see this again, they are in the way of the entrance making it hazardous for everyone. Get rid of this mess or you'll be written up."

As Brent entered the production area, Craig stared in with, "That fucking bitch was just here and ranting about our production area," he went on with a complaint about the third churn and when it's placed how are we to transfer the boxes and the other materials without spillage of frustration. Brent took it all in and just let him rant as he removed the pallet and put it back in the chicken coup.

"Other than the Brenda intervention, how has the day gone?" Brent questioned.

"Great," he lied. "The machine has been running with no problems, and we're ahead of the churn count."

"Okay, let me get started, and I can see I'm going to be changing over after this pallet so everything is good. Have a good night. Oh, yeah, it's snowing so drive carefully."

"Yeah, no fucking problem, fucking snow."

The lab team is also instructed to take the same initiative with all departments going as deep as instructing the maintenance staff as well, this goes into changing of pieces being replaced on machinery or new items being brought in such as tape guns, staples, bolts and pens. Brenda goes as far as making sure that the owner follows her instruction for entrance into the production areas, boots have to be worn and sterilised before entering.

White jackets must be put on and gloves. There are no exceptions.

On one particular day, two weeks after Brent started his employment, "Brent," Brenda asked Brent, "Is that a hair tie on your wrist?"

"Yes?"

"You cannot wear that at work." Brenda continued, "It's the same idea as jewellery, isn't it?"

"No, I don't think so. It sits tight on my wrist. I need it for the pain when it began to tighten from lifting boxes."

"Well, then I suggest you go to the doctor and get a proper wrist brace. That has a potential to brake and contaminate the butter or not be found and end up in the wrapper, or worse wrapped with the butter and sent to retail."

"I don't think that can really happen," Brent said taking it off.

"Excuse me?" she retorted.

Walking away Brent thought to himself, "*Fucking bitch, she really takes things to an extreme.*"

Butter samples were a routine check with every batch. It is taken when in the churn and after being wrapped. Every department does this repetitively through each phase of production to expose any contamination that may happen during the processing of ice cream and the making of butter.

Brenda takes it one step further. Once a week, she will walk to the production area and takes swabs of the inner lining of each churn to make sure there is no build-up of butter to cause bacteria or mould, just to make sure the operators are doing their jobs, keeping the churns clean, and free from butter build-up in the creases. Brenda is relentlessly tormenting when she finds any build-up of butter anywhere on the churns, and she does find it. She makes the operators clean every churn before their shift is finished letting them know she'll be there in the morning to check.

I, the caretaker, am opposed to such extremes; it does not make a healthy environment to work in. It also causes unnecessary hostility. I will go into this; on this one particular morning, Brenda made it a point to show up early and does a churn check. When she found, what she calls unnecessary build-up, she begins her rhetoric of questions, and of course, instead of letting the operator answer for himself, she answers her own questions.

"Why have you let this happen?" she looks at the swab. Then looking sharply at Nate, "I'll tell you why, sloppiness, not observing what you're doing or taking care to what you have in or on your churn. This is neither acceptable nor tolerated by me. I expect better, especially from you. You have had your own production and have a stronger understanding to these machines and to the production of these products.

Seeing this today is bring me to the conclusion to be coming down more often at this time to check on you and what is going on here. I've only started with this at this time but with this discovery, I will make it a continuing event." She left the production area with the swab, but not before turning back with a glaring glance.

"Holy shit! What a fucking bitch!" Nate said aloud for Brent to hear, that's when he started on Brent. "Look at this shit in the corner here why is it there it should be in the chicken coup and the mess behind the wrapper what's all this on the floor?"

There was nothing there really just a few scraps of wrap, staples and some pieces of wood from pallets.

"Why can't you keep it cleaner this is not how it's supposed to be here when Craig is here. Do you see this kind of mass? It must be kept cleaner." Brent looked at him in dismay.

"*Fuck you asshole, you fucking arrogant pig, shut the fuck up*," he thought to himself.

Nate then continued to rant, "Look at the butter boat, why is it so full? It shouldn't be this full why can't you empty it? You should be more aware of what you're doing." Turning away, he went back to watch the timing on the churn.

Brent just went back to the wrapper and maintained what he was doing.

"*This is why I am here, to make right the circumstances that surround the intensity of this building, Issues that are created by individuality, negativity, and position. What happens with this department is missing butter, the amusement here is, Brent, he has only been here a few weeks and is blamed for this. What it is though is Leslie, he goes into the samples and takes one sometimes two, depending on the night in question. There are nights when he just wants to create slightly, all night minor events just to get the crew active and make my night amusing*," the caretaker thought to himself.

"*But he'll only take on these nights as ennui sets in; the nights he does, too, are the extreme happenings when the butter lines up, unwrapped and the box pusher is completely jammed with butter overload and mashed, that is, from Brenda's observations, preventable.*"

Characters:

Brent: Main, new guy
Celina: Brent's girlfriend
Nate: Mixer
Craig: Daytime churn operator
Sherryl: Manager
Sam: Owner
Stan: Evening churn operator
Austin: Evening crew with Brent wrapping operator
Jerry: Daytime wrapping operator
Dan: Maintenance guy
Brenda: Lab tech
Grant: Switched to production from shipping
Karen: Shipping manager

Chapter 12
The Caretaker

Before the building was a butter and ice cream producer, I was the owner, I ran the business like a tight ship. There was no goofing off and no time off everyone employed was here to work, or they were let go.

I would have routine maintenance checks, employee training and cutting test. This was done to keep up our high standards. Even though we were a small business we had a spotless record of no on the job fatalities and, as well, bad product.

I would at times sabotage equipment to have emergency maintenance and shut down the plant. It would only be during slow periods, so it wasn't very often, it was done to keep everything in top running order and everyone would get a needed break.

I was a hands-on boss I would walk the plant daily to make sure everything was being done right, from the cutting to the freezing. All the slaughtering was done as humanely as possible.

Now, my responsibility is this building and with the people who are here. The business has changed and becomes a creamery; my involvement is to oversee all who are here, their character, the temperament, how each person interacts with production as they work together. I find that production is better when there is less agitation when there are misshapes and frustration. Temperaments can get out of control when the machine is acting off balance and that's when the true character of an employee shows.

Most of the action is with the butter wrapper, this machine is very old and finicky, at times it is difficult to keep it in a good registry and that's when frustration and temperament make its incursion with the operator. Most just work through it and handle each incident without emotion, but the ones with less patience, temperament can flare and the day becomes a tangle of offset anger and frustration.

That is when I can make things go into overtime. New employees have this happen until they get a better understanding of the setup and change over and it can get quite messy. Wrap paper can be strewn all over, butter can get into the cavities of the wrapper and along the belt with unwrapped butter as well the box pusher can create a mess with poor aligning and then it can take the operator hours to clean the machine before starting production again.

My minion, Leslie, is good at causing this; he can move things and change positions of items at will and does so regularly. The wrapper and box pusher are his favourite; this area of production brings out the most explosive reactions with employees. All he needs to do is touch the paper as it goes through the first phase with the drop block and its offset and tearing or the registry is skew and needs realigning. This creates a stage of real drama with some of the operators especially if they are new and unfamiliar with the machine.

On this one particular night, a new guy, I think his name was Brent; Leslie caused nothing but problems for him all night. Leslie, just with a touch, caused the paper to skew or jam and it would have to be reset or, the funniest to watch, the butter would not have wrapped, and there would be butter in every cavity and on the belt to be cleaned. This happened at least four times.

Leslie also toyed with the box pusher sometimes preventing a full box but mostly causing a butter overload and that was another mess to be cleaned. Leslie did this simultaneously at times so that both ends would need a major clean and that was fun.

Strangely, though, Brent was very cool about what was going on and stayed his anger but he was very verbal and vulgar, which made the evening entertaining.

"What the fuck," Brent said to himself on the third time setting the registry. "This fucking cunt machine just doesn't want to play right."

As he started the wrapper again, looking over at the boxing pusher, he noticed it was jammed and congested with butter, walking over to empty it and begin cleaning it for the second time, "How the fuck am I going to keep up with this fucking night if all I'm doing is cleaning this fucking cunt machine."

The night operator, who should know more about the machinery, just stood back and watched while Brent went through each tormenting moment of salvation. He is an older smug and unrelenting miserable character with no sense of humour or interactive resolve.

Chapter 13
Possession

I, the caretaker, have one major power, possession. The only thing is it has to be at the right moment of anger and temperament. Some are easy, to cross the threshold, but most are very difficult it must be at a time of weakness but even then there has to be doubt and depression as well. It is a very miss leading assumption that possession is an easy crossing for an entity, but it is quite the opposite.

The one to be crossed into has to be vulnerable and the timing has to be a right opportunity is just a moment of decision and most of the time the crossing is happening coming from a wish of the fault and bad intent. People don't realise how often a wish is based on bad intension and fault but if they thought about it for just one moment, they would not even bring it into a decision. That is when I have all the power and take that moment to cross.

Just as I did with Tom, my first encounter he was a very sad and depressed individual who was looking for a way out. His medication kept him from being vulnerable but when he stopped taking it that's when his darkness began to take over. He fell into a major depression, the beginning of all possession, and spiralled from there. The loss of his job brought in the anger and that's when his wish became expressed.

Of course, it has to be done here, in this building; anywhere else the possession would be impossible, for me with him, but as soon as he knew what was happening with this job it was slipped from thought to verbal expression. That was my moment to cross, and I did.

At first, there is a tantalising dismissal of self as I take over the person being. I begin to see all that they are and wish to be then something miraculous happens, they give in to desire. This is their weakness: what they want and how to get it.

With Tom, it was sabotage; what could he do and how could it be achieved. That's where I step into action.

Once inside the body I am free to move outside the building, anywhere he wishes to be, and that's what I read, the perfect plan of vengeance. My minion, of course, would help to see it through to fruition, but it could only be done once back at the creamery, an easy manipulation; I have now crossed the threshold into Tom and he can only watch as I carry out his disturbance.

Brent, through the night, was constantly battling the wrapper or the pusher that was because Leslie was having fun with Brent. If he, Leslie, wasn't toying with the wrapper, which is his greatest pleasure, he would be disturbing the pusher. The wrapper was the most exciting for him because it would only need a touch from his finger and all hell would break loose. The paper would tear and then the machine would not fill the butter cavities, the sensor that stops the wrapper would sometimes fail or be blocked by wrap, and then the cavities would fill with strictly butter and be pushed onto the conveyer belt which would spread the butter throughout the whole machine.

That's when the real fun started, Leslie would stand back and watch while the person cleaned it for hours, then, after it was reset and functioning, he would do it again. For Brent, this went on throughout the whole night sometimes using both ends as the tormenting tool.

By disturbing the air pressure, he, Leslie, would cause a major binding of butter lining them up on the conveyer and having them be squashed in the pushing machine. When this happens the butter had to be recycled so it would be thrown into a tub to be unwrapped and put back into the butter boat. The butter that was not wrapped had to be re pasteurised, this really kept Leslie and me in quite the euphoric thrill of elation. Every machine and every recipe has its fallibility.

The disturbance is not only done mechanically but with ingredient mixture as well. There was this one time when Nate was mixing two churns of butter. Butter calls for a certain amount of moisture to set right; otherwise, it can turn for hours and remain liquid. In this mixture, Leslie created an over amount of water additive, and this, in turn, prevented the cream from breaking; breaking is the term used when the moisture separates from the cream and it becomes butter.

The moisture or liquid that separates is called buttermilk, this is drained and then what's left is the butter. The butter goes through a wash and then turned to a smooth creamy state then drained again and salt is then added, but for Nate, this went very wrong for some reason and that reason was Leslie.

What he had done was added more cream than was wanted which resulted in a longer breaking time so it would take twice as long to break. Nate was so frustrated by this he started swearing and throwing things, this meant that there was no butter to be wrapped and production was brought to a halt. The wrapping crew had nothing to work with and stood around for the rest of the night with nothing to do, the order to be shipped in the morning was also disturbed and nothing was ready for shipping.

Nate went home in dismay frustrated by the night's turn of events. Bren and Austin could only laugh at the night's event and remark at how they were paid to watch Nate freak out for half the night.

Chapter 14

Brent got to work that night with a raging headache, the night started off well, and the wrapper was working at a good pace and not causing any problems. The pump on the other hand was being choked by water build-up and had to be drained several times. Chad, the backup employee, was onto help with the boxing.

As the pump was compromised early in the evening Brent looked over to see Chad staring at him confused by the noise coming from the pump not knowing what to do. Bent, after pulling the steel shovel out of the butter boat, set it on the shelf and ran over to the wrapper to unplug the airline and bring the feeder back into a full butter capacity so it would be operational again.

The shovel, when Brent went back to the boat, disappeared. Thinking nothing of it he returned to the wrapper to make sure it was operating, then, again, started to look for the shovel.

Thinking Nate had it he went to find him and grab it to continue with working the butter in the boat, but Nate did not have it. Then they all started to hear a bumping noise from the boat.

"I hope the shovel isn't in the butter," said Nate, as Chad started digging into the butter he yelled, "I found it."

"Fuuuuuuuuck!" Nate cried out. "This is going to end the night. We now have to clean out all the butter and the lines."

The shovel looked like it was worked into a fold and cracked. Nate, afraid there were splinters of steel in the butter started pulling butter out of the boat as he did so he was stung by a large splinter of steel and had to attend to it. Chad also suffered the same as he was also pulling butter out of the butter boat.

"The night is over," Nate said in anger. "How could you have let this happen?"

Bent looked puzzled, "I set it on the shelf and it should have been there still, but I must have placed it too close to the butter and it got dragged in."

"Well, now we have to clean out the boat and lines, did any of this butter get into the lines?" Nate asked Brent.

"No, it hasn't been operating after the shovel went missing," replied Brent.

"Well, no matter; everything needs to be cleaned," Nate insisted.

"To be sure the butter is not full of steel splinters."

Brent went and got rework boxes from the storage room and they all started to pull the butter out of the boat. It took four hours and the night was finished.

"I'm so fired, and right after the Stan incident."

"No, you won't be fired, but you may as well go home and come in tomorrow." Nate implied.

"No, I'll stay and help and then go home."

The caretaker, during this whole situation, was standing over them watching, his minion, Less, was behind him and the caretaker questioned, "Did you have anything to do with this?"

"Weeeeell, you know I have the power of object manipulation."

"Yes."

"So, when Brent placed the shovel on the shelf it was close enough to the butter that it only took a little push to get the butterball to grab it and pull it back into the boat, I thought that it is a great trick to play and you would appreciate the gesture. This new guy also needs to learn that attention to where things are placed is very important. Now listen to him he's worried that he may be fired and needs to talk to the manager to secure his position," Less retorted.

"Hum, that's what I admire about you; you're always so mischievous and come up with things I would never have thought of," the caretaker replied.

It took them four hours to clean out the butter from the boat and another two to prepare it for the next morning. Seventy-two boxes of butter had to be trashed, because of this incident. Brent thought for sure he would be fired but it seemed that they are more forgiving than he expected. Brent suffered through the embarrassment of that for the next month.

Chapter 15

It was a breezy night a storm was on the horizon, from the Northwest Rocky Mountains, and being November it had a chill that seemed to go right through a person. Brent, preparing for work decided to go outside to see what the weather was going to be, he didn't trust the weather Chanel being it was located on the eastern province of Ontario, the overhanging clouds.

Let him know to expect a major change than what was predicted on the weather network. After preparing his lunch he grabbed his keys, "I'm gone," he said to Céline.

She walked over to him and kissed him, "Have a good day," and left the house to his car. As he started to drive the snow began to fall it was a twenty-minute drive and pulling into the parking lot the snow was already collecting on the ground.

Entering the building made him realise just how cold the temperature can get in the fall, fast and with no warning. The warmth of the building brought a shiver that went right through the soul and into the head, like when you think you're being followed or watched by an entity. Austin came in just a few moments later, "Holy shit, is it cold out there or what? I'm going to take a few minutes to warm up."

"I know. I went through the same. I've been here for five years, and I'm still not used to the sudden change of temperature. And now that it's snowing; I'm glad I'm driving cause standing to wait for a bus is not going to happen." Brent argued.

"You have a car?" Austin enquired.

"Ya, it's the red ford out in the parking lot but it hasn't been on the road for a year so I don't know how it will run and the heat is going to be an issue, usually that's the first to go when a car sits for a long period of time. Right now it's good but who knows how it will be in a month or so."

"Oh, well I have a car I'm selling, if it doesn't continue to work or something is wrong and you want to buy another one, I can sell this one to you for six hindered, Okay," Austin offered.

"Sure, but let me find out how it turns out before making any decisions alright?" Brent said while changing into his gear.

"Okay. I just want you to know you have another choice if you need to make it."

"Great, but why aren't you driving if you have cars to sell why don't you insure it for yourself?"

"I can't, I owe child support."

"Wow, that's pretty shitty man, I know how that is, my brother owes as well and he's been avoiding it for years. He can't have a license until he pays it off, how much do you owe?" Brent asked.

"Thirteen thousand, but I want to pay it off so I can drive again," Austin implied. They both entered the production room together.

Nothing was out of place or different but they both stopped and looking around Austin turned to Brent and, looking very serious, said, "This place has a ghost. Can you feel it?"

Then Brent said, "I've seen it."

"Nooo. Really? What did he look like?" Austin asked.

Austin is a five-foot-two person of insecurity, a Pilipino; he is highly superstitious, "Where did you see it?" He held up his left arm, "You see that goose bumps. I can feel it all the way up my back. Tell me," he insisted.

"He was standing right in front of me last week. I was working by myself, maintaining this, and as I was standing here, in front of the belt, he was standing right there."

"No way," Austin gasped.

"Ya, his arms were folded, and he just stood there."

"What was he wearing? What did he look like?"

"Well, he wouldn't let me look at him; every time, I looked up to see his face, he disappeared. I can tell you what he was wearing though and how tall he is." Brent put it to question.

"Tell me," Austin demanded.

"He had on a plaid shirt and jeans; he also looked to be about six foot three, with big arms and a gut like he loved his beer." Brent continued, "He stood there for at least two hours it's as though he wanted me to see him but didn't want me to see his face."

"Fucking weird," Austin interjected.

The night began smoothly; the day shift had taken off early, and when they arrived, the wrapper was set for Golden Valley wrap, and halfway through the night, they were to switch to a co-op wrap. Everything was running smoothly until they made the switch to the co-op. For an hour, everything was fine with the wrap; then it started, a few mishaps and tears on the wrapper.

The wrapper and the pusher both went into a binding situation, and they were cleaning both machines. The co-op wrap had been running during this time and tossing butter into the recycling boat as well cleaning both ends of the machine, they began setting the wrap, again, with co-op paper. When they were readying with the wrapper, to start it and putting the pusher back into working order, they were startled by a weird situation.

While setting the box pusher into position, after cleaning it, two levels on the pusher had butter with Golden Valley wrap sitting in it ready to be boxed.

Chapter 16

Grant was a tall lanky person with a touch of ADHD. When he started, his first week was a mix of frustration and anxiety due to accidents caused because he had no experience working with heights on a forklift. Also, the shipping department caused him confusion with the way it was being supervised.

Grants biggest situation was with a full skid of syrup that went off balance; he placed the forks under the skid to the far right and, as a result, lost the full skid. Although it was a heavy loss of product, it was overlooked and forgiven as a rookie's accident. He was surprised at this and appreciated the understanding from management, but it went bad for him again and was again overlooked.

After a few months, in shipping, he asked to be transferred to production. There was too much free time, and he wanted something more active. Nate liked him from the beginning and showed it. He would do small things for him that, when thought about, seemed strangely responsive.

Nate would hang his jacket in the change room or put Grants things in a safer place, to keep from being destroyed or marred, "Brent," Grant started to say, "Nate does things that I'm wondering if he has a different kind of expectation with me."

"Really? What?" Brent enquired.

"I put my jacket down on the stack of skids, and when I went to the change room, there it was, hanging on my locker door on a coat hanger. I'm slightly worried out about it."

"Ya, that is a little bit over the top for someone to take that kind of interest with them. Maybe he's gay, and we don't know. It's like he's in love with you. What you don't want is for him to be inviting you to his house. If that happens, you'd better be on guard for your psyche?"

"I know what you mean he's showing too much interest in my wellbeing and safety. I hope it's just a friend thing cause I'll fuck him up if it goes any further than that."

“Right, just don’t let him get you alone or in a dark area you never know what be on his mind or what his intentions are till it’s acted on.”

“Ya,” Grant agreed.

Grant and Brent were working together that night and Nate was operating the churns. Through the night, they both witnessed some strange carryings-on by Nate.

He would constantly be pulling Grant to the side, for conversation, and staring at him as he and Brent worked the wrapper. Nate would sometimes walk into the production area, through the plastic drapes, and just stand in place starring at Grant. Grant and Brent didn’t know what to think about this.

“It looks like,” Brent began, “you have an admirer.”

“It’s a creepy man. I don’t know what to think but he’s creeping me out, that’s for sure.”

“Then it’s a good thing that Stan is on tonight it makes the night go smoother and without expectations, hey.”

Brent went home after Austin showed up, late again, “Sorry, I’m late, but the bus was late and the one I was on got stuck for about five minutes so it couldn’t be helped.”

“Don’t worry about it. It’s that time. We need some boxes from the back. Can you get them?” Brent asked.

“Sure,” Austin replied.

“I’m out of here,” Brent waved. “See you in the morning.”

“Ya,” Grant nodded.

Brent punched out and went to the change room, got himself together and went to his car. Snow was still falling, and it was heavy on the car so he took his broom out of the back and brushed it off got into it and drove home.

Austin caused a few wrapping disturbances that night and Grant was freaking, before Brent left, when he couldn’t set the wrap correctly a couple of times but other than that the night went fairly smooth.

Chapter 17

It was an extremely cold day and as the evening settled in it got even colder. Brent knew his time at this job was numbered, after the incident with the shovel, it didn't feel right anymore and being there felt like he was counting days before he would be dismissed. Getting ready for work, he looked outside to see what he would be driving in, either snow or ice.

"Hey, hun," his girlfriend questioned, "when are you going?"

"I'm going to leave earlier. I don't know what the roads are like so I'm leaving early and taking my time."

"Ya, that's a good idea," she agreed.

Again the mischievous behaviour of Leslie has played a factor in the happenings with the butter boat. As Brent walked into the production area, he was surprised by another incident that had happened earlier in the day. The day crew had just finished the clean-up of the boat involving another shovel, again being caught in the butter and destroyed.

"Hey, Brent, you won't believe what happened," Grant said to Brent as he walked into the production area.

"What?" Brent asked.

"The same thing you went through last month happened to me. The plastic mixing stick had gotten into the butter, somehow. And production had to be stopped, and the butter removed and treated with the same caution because the augers would slice and fracture the tool and mix the pieces into the butter. All the butter that is in the boat would be discarded and thrown into the trash. It was the plastic shovel, but we still had to clean everything out. The plastic chips have gotten into the whole mix so it's scraped and in rework, to be sent to the dump," Grant expressed.

"Holy shit, how?"

"I set the shovel on the butter boat shelf, and it, somehow, ended up in the boat and mixed with the butter so after fishing it out we had to do the same thing when it happened to you. We're just finishing up and putting it all back together now."

Craig looked up and smiled. "Well, it's quite obvious that this is not a one-time thing. It's one thing to have it happen once but if it happens twice, there's a problem so obviously. Nothing can be placed on the shelf, and we must make sure that this does not happen again."

"Well, it validates what I said happened to me at least."

Grant then went over to the shelf and put his hand on it, "Ya, just as I thought, it vibrates, that's what caused it to happen both times." Grant exclaimed.

But I, the caretaker, know better Les, my minion, is the culprit here. He, with his ability to move objects, pushed the shovel into the boat, Grant continued with his explanation, "All I did was set it down on the shelf to get the hose, I was gone for just a moment, and when I got back it was gone."

"I know," said Brent. "It happens fast and with no explanation. How do you prevent something from happening when you're gone for just a few seconds? It shouldn't be that fast."

Again, as they turned on the compressor, they all heard it. It sounded like laughter, looking at each other Craig said, "That's the strangest thing I've heard this compressor do, and it's been a few times doing this, but it sounds like it's laughing."

Looking around at everyone, "Hey?" Craig enquired.

Brent had at least an hour to mull around before the wrapper would be ready to set up and function so he began pulling out the wrapping paper to be used and boxes that were going to be needed for his shift. He would be on this shift by himself, with Nate, operating the churns.

Chapter 18

Golden Valley? Puzzled both of them stood looking at the stack ready to be boxed, turning to look at each other they said in unison, "How could this happen?" Brent questioned.

"There's no way, we've been wrapping with the co-op for at least an hour and cleaned the wrapper and pusher two or three times, there is no way."

"Well, I would say this makes it official, doesn't it. There's a ghost here; this has no other explanation." Brent suggested.

As I stood there watching them go through this question of circumstance, I could only chuckle at the thought of how right they are, but I had nothing to do with this one either. Less has his tricks, and on this one even I don't know how he pulled this one. Leslie was behind Stan laughing. Then he got up and walked over to me, "So do you want to know how I did this one?"

"Yes, of course, this is one of the freakiest things you've ever pulled."

"I know, and it can't be done again for about three months."

"Why?" the caretaker asked him, questioning his honesty.

"Because I have only a few defiance events in any given year."

"Who are you defying?" the caretaker asked.

"It's not who it's, and what it is, is contingency, an unforeseen event. It's like working with mirrors, a smokescreen, by fucking up the wrapper and having them clean and reset it. I could take several stakes of wrapped butter with the Golden Valley wrap on them and refracting the light so they don't see what's right in front of them."

Leslie began explaining, "It's like a mirror effect, instead of seeing what's there they see the floor."

"But how did you get them into the pusher so perfect?" the caretaker questioned.

“The power of persuasion, with the thought of wanting them to be there, they were. Like when I move objects, the same with you, when you move objects as well but you have to know how to refract and I don’t think you have that ability.”

Leslie impressed the caretaker with that image. From that moment on, and for the next month, things went well with little or no mishaps.

Chapter 19
Possession

I, the caretaker, have one major power, possession. The only thing is it has to be at the right moment of anger and temperament. Some are easy, to cross the threshold, but most are very difficult it must be at a time of weakness but even then, there has to be doubt and depression as well. It is a very miss leading assumption that possession is an easy crossing for an entity, but it is quite the opposite.

The one to be crossed into has to be vulnerable and the timing has to be a right opportunity is just a moment of decision and most of the time the crossing is happening coming from a wish of the fault and bad intent. People don't realise how often a wish is based on bad intension and fault but if they thought about it for just one moment, they would not even bring it into a decision. That is when I have all the power and take that moment to cross.

Just as I did with Tom, my first encounter he was a very sad and depressed individual who was looking for a way out. His medication kept him from being vulnerable but when he stopped taking it that's when his darkness began to take over. He fell into a major depression, the beginning of all possession, and spiralled from there. The loss of his job brought in the anger and that's when his wish became expressed.

Of course, it has to be done here, in this building; anywhere else the possession would be impossible, for me with him, but as soon as he knew what was happening with this job it was slipped from thought to verbal expression. That was my moment to cross, and I did.

At first, there is a tantalising dismissal of self as I take over the person's being. I begin to see all that they are and wish to be then something miraculous happens, they give in to desire. This is their weakness, what they want and how to get it.

With Tom it was sabotage, what could he do and how could it be achieved? That's where I step into action.

Once inside the body I am free to move outside the building, anywhere he wishes to be, and that's what I read, the perfect plan of vengeance. My minion, of course, would help to see it through to fruition, but it could only be done once back at the creamery, an easy manipulation, I have crossed the threshold with Tom and he could only watch as I carried out his interference.

Two months after he was hired, Brent, arriving at work, saw as an EMS was leaving the parking lot. Several police cars were parked outside the building and, as Brent entered, he was confronted by Sherryl, the manager, and told there is no work tonight; the building is closed for the rest of the day and tomorrow. Just then Chad was being led out, in handcuffs, and put into a cruiser.

"There has been a terrible situation and I think the police are going to want to question you at some point either today or tomorrow so stick around and I'll let you know in a while when they want to speak to you," Sherryl said to Brent and the others that were still in the building.

Brent was there for about two hours before being questioned by a detective; letting him know what he had overheard during his first month of employment, between the two individuals.

Brent learned from Jerry that Chad had stabbed Charlie several times, just before he arrived, for calling him a crack head and that his wounds were quite severe, and it's not known if he is alive or if he will survive the attack. The good thing is Charlie had been training Nate, before going on holiday, so he would be able to take over until he had recovered and is ready to return to work.

Arriving at work, after two days off, Brent was told that Charlie didn't survive; he was pronounced DOA as he arrived at emergency. That left Nate to take over the mixing.

There is knowing and not knowing and I, the caretaker, know, for I have the gift. There is a moment when a person is struggling with emotions and they lose all sense of self. That is when they are vulnerable to the intervention of the soul.

In other words, I can enter their body; any spirit with this ability can do this, not all have it, actually very few, and take control of who they are. With this as an opportunity there is a spectacular result, the spirit knows the person's past present and can change the future of events acting on their most hidden evil. In this case, with Chad, it is the murder of Charlie for his assault on his character and mindset.

When I first entered Chad, it took a moment of forcible thought to take control. Chad had done so much acid and mixed it with MDA that even Chad had no control over thought or reason; he was like a walking contradiction in thought and in action. I had to break him from this confusion, bring his evil to the surface, and set him on the path to self-destruction.

Chad always carries a knife; it's a lock blade, a very effective killing tool. Pulling it from his back pocket Chad opened the blade and with it, in his left hand, waited until Nate had left the mixing room.

Nate was being trained by Charlie to take his position when he had time off or was sick. You see any activity that is done by a person, out of character, out of reason and out of responsibility to job agenda or routine is by possession. As Nate went through the door to the lunchroom Chad, I, entered the mixing room.

"Hey," Chad motioned, Charlie just looked at him and said, under his breath, to himself.

"*Fucking crackhead*," Chad heard this; or rather I made Chad hear this with telepathy. We, as entities, have the power to read the minds of others, as; we do possess the souls of the troubled and confused.

"I told you what would happen if you called me that again," Chad said angrily, stabbing Charlie in the throat three times, then lower, to the chest, below the heart, and then in the abdomen and torso. Chad's madness is from me his insanity is my temperament, as the caretaker, I become Chad's proprietor in crime and Charlie becomes Chad's subject.

Chad then, as though nothing had happened, left the mixing room and went back to the boxes he had been labelling for the yoghurt milk, not seeing that he had blood all over his arms and hands and getting it all over the jugs he was working with.

Nate, discovering Charlie, called 911 desperately, "We have an emergency my co-worker is dying we need EMS here now!" kneeling down to check his pulse he found that Charlie was still alive, knowing not to move the person he started talking, "You're going to be fine help is on its way and you'll be okay."

I the caretaker directed this with Chad and when I left his body he went into a state of incoherence and amnesia, this state of mind blinds the person from seeing what they have on them and their focus is on the task and not their surroundings. Chad was in this trance like state when the police arrived and took him into custody; he had no recollection of the incident and denied that it ever happened.

"We would like to talk to the witnesses and get their statements of what they saw," the police instructed Sheryl.

"Okay, but most were at their places working and the only person who found Charlie was Nate. He called the EMS and your team followed after they arrived. So I don't think you're going to get much from anyone, it was done so fast and without witnesses. You're going to get what you need from Chad and from what I've just heard from him, he has no recollection," Sheryl exclaimed.

"Well, we need to put something down in writing so can we talk to Nate?" The policeman enquired.

"Yes, of course, Nate? Has anyone seen, Nate?" Sheryl asked.

"He's in the dressing room at his locker changing," answered Brent.

"Can you go get him, the officer here needs to ask him a few questions about the incident?"

"Ya," Brent went in and told Nate that the police want to talk to him, he said okay and said, "They can wait till I'm finished," when he was ready, he went out and found the officer, "What I need to know is what you saw," the policeman asked.

"Well, it isn't much I first saw him when I arrived and he was good staying to himself, but then, now, as I was going to the washroom, I saw that he was lying on the floor and there was blood everywhere I had my phone in my pocket so I called 911, I don't know who call the police but you guys arrived almost at the same time," Nate recounted. "I didn't even know who had done this until I saw Chad being led out in handcuffs."

"So, basically there are no witnesses, not that we need them, but it will only be he said she said in court if he pleads, not guilty," the officer retorted.

"Ya, I guess?"

After everyone was questioned, that needed to be, and the police were satisfied and gone Sheryl shut down the plant and sent everyone home and thinking to herself, "*This has been going on a lot lately and I'm beginning to wonder if this place is haunted, and the surprising thing is Sam is always gone when these things happen. As well he goes out and finds a new interest and expects me to participate. This has to end at some point or at least find some solace in this. I'll just ride it out for now but it's got to have some intervention or resolve and soon.*"

Sheryl went back to her office and began preparing to leave when Sam walked in.

Chapter 20

The day was spent toiling with the idea that Brent should start looking for another job. It was a Wednesday, and so much has happened that this one was beginning to feel like all the rest, temporary.

It wasn't just the shovel incident but the way he was being shifted around and his hours cut. It was snowing and cold so he spent most of the day cleaning and preparing his lunch for the graveyard shift, it usually was made of leftovers from the previous day or two, sandwiches as well as fruit and sometimes cookies.

Nate was on the churning that night, he is the company backup, when there is an absence of an employee, he steps in to take the position. He knows four different positions, to fill the void when someone is sick or on holiday. Being the brain of the operations he held an arrogance that set him apart from everyone, he could and does tell anyone and everyone what he expected from them and how the place should be running.

Brent, when he got to the creamery, discovered he was on his own working solids, "Fuck..."

His time on this was awkward. When he worked with a partner it went well but on his own, nothing went right. It was a sloppy mess, and only got worse through the night, he would start up the machine and it would run well for about five boxes then jam. And that's when the strain of the machine began.

Brent began with spraying the feeder line with hot water, to free up the butter, but that didn't work, most of the time. "This is what they fucking showed me why is it not working for fuck sakes?" he questioned himself aloud. "This is crap."

When he finally got it going, it was a butter bath. On the floors on the walls, on the machine, butter everywhere. The butter came out of the feeder in liquid form, and there was nothing he could do about it. The line would block, and he would be heating it up again, to get the flow happening, but when it would free from the line the butter was liquid and there was butter everywhere so most of the night was spent cleaning and trying to get the machine to feed properly.

Nate was watching and, standing there with his arms folded, "What the fuck?"

"I know," said Brent, "I'm doing exactly what I was shown and this is how it comes out. I don't know what I'm doing wrong but it's a mess," he said without expression.

"Well, I've got three dumps in the boat that's how far behind you are with it. There's no way you're going to catch up."

"Nothing I can do about it, it's not changing with whatever I do."

The next morning he was so far behind that the head of the churns asked, "What's going on?"

That's when Brent showed him how it was functioning and even with his intervention, Nate, it continued to act in the same manner. "Why the fuck is this happening?"

"I know, this is just fucked and I wanted this night to go smooth but now look it's just a mess and I'm not going to be any better than tonight." Brent went home in dismay.

This went on for two nights, then they brought Austin in to work with Brent, and it all went smooth. "What was happening?" questioned Austin.

"I don't know, I've been doing it the same way you just did it and it all stops then when I heat the pipes it comes out all sloppy and there's butter everywhere, I don't know why it's doing that but It only acts right when I'm working with you so I think it's just conspiring against me." Austin chuckled and shrugged.

Chapter 21

It was known that Sam and Sheryl spent the long weekend together, they were seen down at the Roundhouse pub, not in a passionate way but as a casual interlude. They also left together, which shouldn't bring in questions of any relationship everyone knew Sheryl's sexuality and the person she is with has been a long-time association. Still, suspicion and rumour began to arise with the idea that there was more going on between the two of them than thought in the past.

"Sheryl, I have an event I want you to participate in," Sam always talked in code, using different words to describe what he is setting up for and wanting Sheryl to be a part of, "This weekend is a long one and I've been observing a subject of interest and I think you'll like it as well."

Sheryl knew that as Sam is getting older his strength and his size doesn't always let him get the advantage of the person he has been tracking. "I want you to meet me at the Roundhouse and we'll discuss what we can do to remedy this situation and gain control over it, say 9:00 pm?"

"Okay," she agreed, not really in the mood of what to expect, but it's like when things happen at the plant it creates an impression with Sam and he gets excited with his intention expecting Sheryl to feel the same way.

"9 then." The only thing Sheryl gets is a curiosity of who he has intended to persuade to do this too.

She knows that she is the key to make it happen without her it would go into a questionable situation but when she's there it always goes smooth and the end results always favour Sam. When she got there, she saw him sitting in his usual spot, it didn't matter what bar or pub or lounge they went to he would always be in the back corner, behind the lights, so he was more in shadow and less likely to be observed.

Walking over to join him, "Hey," she greeted him casually.

"Your late," he replied abruptly.

“Well, this is not what I had on my agenda for this weekend and I’ve had to make changes to accommodate you with this interlude.”

“All’s good, he isn’t here yet anyway and we can sit and talk about how this will be done and where.”

“You always chose the same place, so, where is never the issue and how, well that depends on the person, doesn’t it. Do you have what is needed? I don’t want this to go badly, remember what happened the last time,” she implied.

“Yes, I do, and yes I have it.”

What she was asking for is GHB Sheryl has a very cute way of expressing herself, when confronting a subject. She goes into a young girlish approach to distract him and drug his drink, this one was no different. She usually has several drinks, with the person of interest, and gains his confidence then, after a couple of hours, slips the dose into his drink. Everyone has seen them together for most of the night and with her sleaze tease she always keeps him interested and not wanting to leave, it works every time.

When the subject shows signs of readiness that’s when Sam walks up, as a complete stranger, and offers to give her a hand with her date, together they carry him out to the car. Dragging him to the back seat of the car they take him to the usual place of abode they drag him in and tuck tape him to the bed, chair or table, for this venture it is a bed. That’s when Sheryl leaves; she doesn’t stay for the ascendancy but waits to be summoned to dispose of the body.

Chapter 22

The technicians, in the lab, were always overstepping their position, with maintenance; and other departments believed they could tell them how to prepare each item before bringing any item into the production area. That way there was no contamination while doing their job. Everything they applied in production had to be sterilised, sanitised and approved by the lab techs before use.

Brenda oversaw this extreme and expected complete cooperation, and they did. Bolts were boiled, and tools steamed replacement pieces were steamed, everything that was brought in went through some type of pre-sterilisation. Even the chicken coup, where the boxes and plastic containers were stored, had an air purification system so they were kept from funguses and moisture.

The night crew had a more relaxed shift because Brenda was only there during the day, so they tended to leave out some of the expectations while she was not around. Maintenance also became more relaxed with the procedure, of sterilisation, as well.

On this one particular night, Brenda stayed late. It was just after the second incident of a shovel slipping into the butter boat, It happened in the same manner as the first incident.

When the new shovel was introduced, Brenda, being vigilant, stayed to observe how it was being used and how it could possibly have ended up in the boat.

The night crew had left the production area for a break, Nate, for a smoke and the rest of the crew for food, Brenda had stayed behind. Alone, in the production area, she put the shovel on the shelf of the butter boat to see if she could recreate the incident. Walking around to the switch, behind the boat, she decided to make an observation of the churn to see if Stan could have avoided his demise with the incident of the churn falling on top of him.

As she was looking inside, Leslie, my minion, noticed her bending over and reaching out with her left hand, to observe and test the consistency. That's when he, Leslie, took action; she was slightly off-balance while reaching, so Leslie, moving the butter table and bumped her with it.

The butter table is heavy, seven hundred pounds, and always set several feet in front of the churn when getting ready to dump into the butter boat, and this was a small batch of one thousand two hundred pounds. When the table bumped her, strangely, the same occurrence happened again. Her right arm was held behind her back, to maintain a better balance, and when bumped her right arm automatically flew out to grab something to prevent falling into the churn.

Grabbing the switch box she accidentally turned on the churn as she fell into the butter, in the churn, and was caught in the momentum of the motion and pulled into the butter mass, snapping her neck immediately.

As the churn rotated, she became entangled in its mass and slammed, with the mass of butter, on the bottom of the churn every time it did a full rotation. This went on for ten minutes until Nate came back into the production area and noticed the churn spinning.

"What the fuck?" he asked himself and ran over to check it out. He noticed the butter boat had been moved and was just a few feet from the mouth of the churn, as well, when he got to the churn and turned it off wondering where Brenda had gone to. Thinking she just left and was preparing to go home he wheeled the butter table into the churn, turning it on, to load the butter onto the table, with the first slam of butter onto the table he saw Brenda, she was engulfed in butter and not moving. Overcome with shock and disbelief, he just stood there and stared.

"How the fuck…" he said aloud, taking a few steps backwards; he tripped and fell on his ass.

Hearing the door to the production area open and some voices, he knew it was Austin and Brent, "Hey, Brent," Nate called out, "call 911, NOW," Brent had his phone in hand and, as he and Austin walked to the churn, Brent pressed the emergency app on the phone.

Approaching, he and Austin saw Brenda laying on the table. "What the fuck?" they both said in unison.

"How could this happen?" They all stood there looking at the churn and each other in question.

Nate snatched the phone from Brent and talking excitedly, "We need an EMS down at Golden Valley, now. We've had an incident, and I think she's dead," he said with uncertainty and a quiver of malady.

"Brent, you don't mind if I call Sheryl about this, do you?"

"No, go ahead; she needs to be informed," Brent added.

Nate had Sheryl on the line and explained to her what had just happened, that he had called for an EMS, and the police were on the way, but he felt that she needed to be here. "I really think you should be here," Nate said in an abrupt tone; he has that typical arrogance of a self-righteous narcissist.

Sheryl agreed and said she'd be down as soon as possible. Nate handed Brent's phone back to him and motioned to stand back. The police had just arrived, and Austin was letting them in, as he was doing that the EMS arrived and entered as well.

"What have we got?" asked the EMS team. They all stood around the churn and looked inside, on the butter table lay Brenda.

"Does anyone know how this occurred?" The police asked Nate.

"No, I was the one who found her, when I didn't see her in the area, I thought she had left to prepare to go home. I had also, when I walked in, noticed that the churn was turning, and I know I had to be turned off, emptied and transferred to the boat. When I approached the churn and turned it off, I put the table into the churn and rotated it with a load of butter and that's when Brenda fell onto the table." Nate explained in a monotone.

Sheryl was taken to the side by police and in conversation as well. There was nothing that she could add, and they knew that she arrived after they had gotten there. They just stuck to general questions of who was on and how they could get a hold of her if they needed any more information.

Chapter 23
Churn

There are plans to have a third churn brought in before the end of the year. Halfway through Brent's third month of employment, it was sitting in the pasteurising area, by the door to the waste cans, outside.

As the third churn was being placed, there were several things that had to be addressed; one the area chosen would limit the walking space and compromise the entrance to the storage room, referred to as the chicken pen. Two; the floor in the spot is uneven and the churn had to be stabilised in some way, shimmed, ground, or some way with a concrete additive to level the placement.

This added more time to the installation and took weeks of planning and work, but it was finally put into place.

"Hey," said the supervisor "how's it going?" he asked.

"Well, we are about to mount the churn, but we thought we could wait till tomorrow."

"No, I would like it done before you go that way, we can know how stable it is and whether we need to rebalance the machine as well."

"Okay, but that will bring me into an overtime situation and I want double time none of this time and a half shit."

"Alright, just don't make it last all night."

"Yeah, yeah, I'm not interested in an all-night thing. I'll be out a here as quick as possible."

"Great, see you tomorrow, and you know where to be, right?"

"Yeah, the sinner's domain at 9:00 am."

"That's right and no excuses for no show either."

"Right, fuck you too."

All of this set a tone of weirdness for the night and Brent felt it as he entered the building. Austin had gone on holiday for a few weeks so Stan and Brent were alone for the night working the churns. It started, though, on solids but when Brent started the second skid the feeder jammed and wouldn't fill the boxes.

"Hey, Stan. This machine isn't working."

"It will once I put another churn into the boat." The boat is a tub with augers.

That feeds the lines for filling the boxes or the wrapper lines. Brent had to wait at least a half-hour before this happened so he proceeded to heat the lines and keep trying to fill the box, which turned out to be in vain. After Stan had dumped the next churn into the boat Brent went back to the solids and turned it on, the pressure and box holder all worked but as soon as the box was set to be filled it just stayed in one place motionless.

That was the beginning of the strangeness that overwhelmed the evening. It was a series of incidents that began with the solids, after an hour of trying to get it to work they decided to call Craig, he suggested that they change over to unsalted Golden Valley and box them until the boat was done. Then they could continue with celestials salted for the rest of the night, that's when the second weird occurrence happened.

While making the change from unsalted to salted, Brent went through the procedures and did everything in proper order, but as he started the machine, it began wrapping but the butter was not being fed onto the paper. Stan walked over and observed that the sheer bolt had snapped and told Brent to call Dan and ask him to come and fix it if he can.

"You realise I'm off work, right," Dan interjected.

"Yeah, but if you don't put in the sheer bolt we have to shut down for the night."

"Right, and we can't have that happen can we," Dan agreed.

"No, Stan is already pissed that we've been shut down for twenty minutes at this time, so is it possible? Please say yes," Brent pleaded. Dan agreed and said he would be there in the hour and have it complete before 11:00 pm. This was around 9:00 pm, and things didn't get better from that point on. When Dan arrived, after assessing the situation, he began looking for the pieces and explained that the washers had to be found, Brent eventually found them, one on the floor and the other camouflaged on the bottom of the cam.

"Great, now things get easier from here, we can get started on the completion of the bolt insertion," he exclaimed.

Stan was also involved in the final phases. With the next two churns, "I'm not going to stick around to dump them I'm going to let the day crew do that." That's when it went terribly wrong.

As Stan returning to the churns, to make them ready for the day crew, let out a wail "Aaaaaaah…"

As Dan and Brent turned to look, they witnessed the churn, closest to the butter boat, doing something rather odd. It appeared to be turning properly but was swinging a filler pipe towards the ceiling. Tearing out the other filler lines; on the ceiling, it swung around jamming on the floor.

That's when things got really interesting. Stan, still lying on the floor, had been knocked unconscious, and when the filler line hit the floor, again, the Churn began to rip from its foundation snapping the bolts in the floor and started to teeter down on top of Stan, where he was still lying. This all happened in a matter of seconds and all Dan and Brent could do was watch.

The Churn, still rotating, fell on top of Stan's lower abdomen and began rolling up his body. Because it was filled with liquid cream inertia kept it in motion. It rolled right over the top of him, crushing him, pausing for a moment, at his chin, and then continued to crush his head.

It continued to roll into the butter boat and stopped. As Dan ran around to shut off the Churn, he realised that it, during all of the movement and leaving its position on the floor, had pulled the electrical wiring from the back of the box, on the Churn, which had made it free to roll over Stan and bump into the butter boat. Dan, seeing Stan in the condition, threw up all over the floor.

"We have to call 911," Brent, ran to his locker and, finding his phone, dialled 911.

After the investigation, it was assessed that as Stan was returning to the churns, he slipped on some butter that was left on the floor and, when reaching out to prevent himself from falling, he grabbed the switch stand and turned on the churn that still had the fill line placed on it.

Stan was thrown backwards and landed on the floor, between the churn and the butter boat. The churn, as it began to turn. With the fill line still attached, tore out the rest of the fill lines on the ceiling and continued until the fill line, still attached to it, hit the floor.

The churn and the rotation machine began to tumble to the right, where Stan had been thrown on his back. The churn and the mounting fell over onto Stan's torso and, because the churn was still in motion, it continued to roll over the top of Stan.

That's how it was written in the police report, but it was a whole different story according to Leslie. Stan had gotten back to the churn and, while walking to the view window, to see how much water was in the churn, Leslie tripped him and pushed Stan, making sure he rolled under the churn.

Stan, reaching out to grab something to prevent the fall accidentally turned on the churn, this was an unforeseen happening that Leslie didn't expect to occur, and with that everything went into a secondary motion of disaster.

After calling the EMS and police Don called Sheryl, "Hey, sorry to call you so late in the evening but we've had a major situation and I think you need to be here."

"Can you let me know what it is?" she asked.

"Stan is dead; it was a freak accident with the churn. I think you need to see it instead of being told." Dan imposed.

"I'll be down in half an hour I have to get dressed and bring myself into readiness," she implied.

"Okay," Dan retorted, when she arrived the police were still there, but the EMS was gone, the blood, still on the floor, was draining into the subfloor drain. The churn had to be knocked over to pull Stan from beneath it, being the stand that supported the churn came to rest on his chest.

"Please tell me how this happened," she asked with a remorseful tone.

"I don't know Brent and I just watched as it did this, we don't know how or why, it just did," Dan said expressionlessly.

Dan and Brent came to the conclusion that inertia played a major part in this with the weight of the butter, still inside, and the weight of the Churn, as well, there was no stopping the event from happening.

"The police have taken both our statements and we would like to go home, or do you want more from us tonight."

"No, you both can go; I'll have a clean-up crew in tonight and close the creamery for tomorrow as well," she said.

"Okay, thanks. Good night; see you in two days," Dan expressed.

Brent also said good night and went home. When he got home his girlfriend asked what he was doing home so early, he explained the situation and told her he also had tomorrow off with pay, "That's so cool," he said to her before getting ready for bed, She wanted to have sex but Brent exclaimed how horrific it was and couldn’t bring himself to it. He went to bed, and in the morning, they made love.

Chapter 24

It was early morning, Nate had just got out of bed his significant other was also rising after the night of passion, “It’s going to be a day of newness I have to train a new guy on the mixes and work the churns so it’s a busy day and possibly into a late day, around seven or eight.”

“Well, that’s the norm isn’t it,” replied Jacque.

“I didn’t sign up for this it just landed in my lap as people quit and were fired, but it is what it is and I just roll with it.”

“That’s what I’ve been doing since I met you, rolling with it,” Jacque gave a snicker and nudged Nate. He turned to put water into the coffee maker and started with some toast before beginning the eggs for breakfast.

Because of losses suffered at the creamery, Jerry was sent to mixing he had on the job training at another creamery, with the mixer, before coming to Golden Valley, and after Charlie’s death, he was sent to spend time with Nate to learn the recipes and agenda of preparation as well as clean-up.

Nate was to stay with the churning; he used to work two jobs at a time, but in this case, he would be just keeping an eye on Jerry and to step in, whenever there was a question or confusion, to make sure everything was in working out.

“So how are things going here,” enquired Nate?

“Great, I’ve got this one all most complete it will be ready for the silo before the afternoon,” Jerry was to start with the chocolate yoghurt mix for bottling it needed to be ready before 1 o’clock so the bottling could start by 1:30 or 2:00 in the afternoon.

“That’s great you’re on time and it smells like it should so it will be the right consistency and the right texture,” Nate observed.

Jerry went down to the ice cream section to let Ingrid know it would be an hour before she could start bottling. Ingrid began preparation, directing the crew to begin labelling and making boxes.

Nate went back to the churns to see what stage they were at knowing one was ready to be dumped into the butter boat, "This should go smoothly tonight."

It was just coming on to twelve, and the day crew was just making a change, with the wrap to Golden Valley, the company's name brand. There was a big order to be shipped the next day, and they had to make at least seven skids that night.

There was a complication throughout the day. The wrapping machine was constantly tearing the last paper wrap, and they couldn't figure out why, but as they were setting the Golden Valley, it was discovered that one of the push keys was offset and had to be readjusted. This took several hours, and now Nate had two dumps in the boat, and the day crew was behind that meant the night crew had to work harder to complete the seven skids, but it could be done. Seven skids were the usual norm depending on the function of the wrapper and the pusher, if all went well the order would be ready for shipping in the morning.

As the evening crew began to arrive Cliff went over the night's agenda and then explained what the problems were during the day shift and that the order had to be completed that night for shipping in the morning. "Ya, this is an important shipment it goes out first thing in the morning."

"There should be no problems since you fixed the finger, Austin and I can usually handle it pretty well and get at least seven skids done through the night," replied Brent. That night did go smoothly and the shipment was ready for the next day.

Chapter 25
Sam and Sherryl

The evening was blustery and raining and Sherryl was to meet with Sam at the nearby pub for drinks and to discuss the routine of the coming weekend, she was readying herself to leave when she got a call from the creamery.

"Hello, it is Cliff. I just wanted to check in and let you know that everything was fine when I left, but, there have been some strange happenings through the day that have left me with concern with the night shift. The churns have been shutting off at irregular periods and the butter tray has been moving on its own, at times, significantly.

"Just to give you an idea, I left the tray by churn one and went for lunch and when I returned it was in front of the water silo, now, no one was in the production area at the time and it's unusual to have it placed there during the breaking stage of the cream. I know the floors are uneven and it does move on its own at times but to have the tray move to that extreme is not usual. So, just to make you aware that I'm uneasy about tonight's production and that maybe you should call at some point just to make sure things are okay."

"Ya, sure, I'm about to have a meeting with Sam so after that I will call to find out how things are."

"Okay, sounds good. Have a good night then."

"You as well, see you tomorrow." They both ended the call.

And Sherryl decided to walk to the pub, being it was so close, and she had no other plans.

Arriving at the pub, she noticed Sam was already there, joining him he mentioned, "I have taken the liberty of ordering you a drink; it will be here in a moment."

She pulled her chair and sat down, "As you know there have been a few incidents over the past six months that have brought major attention to our creamery. This doesn't stop anything I have plans and you will accompany me this time as well."

Her drink was set in front of her, and she killed it with one gulp, as he went onto say, "We are being watched but it's only due to the incidents that have been occurring at the creamery, so it just gives more intrigue to the game."

"It's inevitable that you'll be caught, you know this, right." She replied, and went onto say, "You also know that my part in this is just to dispose of the remains I have no part in the act of what you do."

"You have nothing to worry about, I have taken care of the paperwork and if or when it all comes to a conclusion you will be exonerated and obtain ownership of the creamery. My lawyer as all the affirmations and confirmations on file included is a sworn statement of your innocence and my confession."

He ordered another round and continued to say, "Just to be clear, I have no family so you don't have to worry about someone challenging or trying to arbitrate my decision it is solid."

"Well, It seems you've made your decision about the weekend so I'll be on my way and don't call me until you know exactly what the game plan is," she said sternly.

Leaving, she grabbed her second drink and finished it with intensity then put on her coat and left. Sherryl returned home, where she found her significant other waiting, "Where have you been?" she asked.

"Oh, just had a drink with my boss and a bit of a meeting, going over the circumstances of the past few months and trying to figure out a way to prevent reoccurrences," she lied.

"I hope things get better there it's strange for it to be happening in such a short time span I'm surprised the police aren't doing a more in-depth investigation."

"Oh, they are watching and Sam thinks he's being followed but these are just circumstances that are not predictable and can only be tied to overwork or disorders." They both went to bed and prepared for the next day.

Chapter 26

Craig had also, just recently, been trained to operate the churns and on this day, he would be working the graveyard shift, “I hate this shift it’s always a twelve-hour shift unless something goes wrong, and the churns have to shut down,” he said aloud getting ready for the night. “I wonder who’s going to be on.”

The day was bitter and cold and that meant the night wasn’t going to be any different, “At least I’m inside,” he said, talking to his wife.

Craig is a short dumpy character but with a strong body and work ethic. He would always be complaining about all the overtime they expected them to carry out, without being asked, and let everyone know about it, “Hey, Grant.”

“Hey.”

“Ready for the night?”

“Yeah, but I’m not sure about a few things.”

“Like what?” Craig enquired.

“The pusher for the boxes, it keeps messing up and makes everything completely frustrated and I’m not good with it.”

“Well, just go with it should work out okay but if you have any problems I’m here to help as well.”

“Okay.”

They both went to their areas and began working and it started right after the tenth box the butter started lining up and it became a cluster of squashed butter.

After turning off the machine, Grant started tossing butter into the boat and cleaning off the butter stuck to the push bands. As Grant started the wrapper, the paper then began to tear, and there was a mess again. This time, it was on the conveyer belt with unwrapped butter and in the pockets of the wrapper, where the butter is dropped into the wrap.

“Fuuuuuuuck, what, is this machine on crack?”

He then began the arduous task of cleaning the wrapper and belt, all the cleaning takes time and puts the wrapping behind by hours.

Leslie couldn't help but laugh each time. He disturbed the production, with Grant. Grant was so irate that with every incident, he freaked.

Leslie's disturbance went on for the first few hours of the shift but then stopped, just before ten, and the night went on with no troubles or frustration.

Chapter 27

The next night was humid and stormy Grant was working the wrapper alone, again, and Nate was operating the churns. As grant was in the process of changing the wrap, Leslie, my minion, would touch the wrap intermittently, as it was being fed into the wrapper, causing the paper to tear and the machine to jam. Leslie did this for hours, Grant, screaming, was not happy about the situation, frustrated and losing his temper, "This fucking machine…why, why, why?"

Once the machine was set it ran smooth for the next few hours then Leslie would cause another jamming of the butter wrapping production line, but this time it was at the other end. The boxing of the butter is a very time conscious process. Every thirty seconds the operator had to be in position to capture the next stacked butter as it was being pushed into the box, if the person wasn't ready this could cause a miner mess that could be left till after break.

Leslie loved how Grant, in his animated rage, would have swearing fits and punch things. Leslie would laugh long and hard as would I, standing back, watching his genius as he toyed with the machine and I took pleasure watching him creating mischievous tricks. Grant got so frustrated, after the sixth incident, he had to turn off the wrapper and go outside for a smoke.

"There's no need for you to get so worked up, it's just a machine and it's old so it's going to have problems and tonight it seems to have more than usual." Nate said with compassion.

He then walked over to Grant and started rubbing his shoulders, "Wow, you've really worked up some tension, just relax and let the night go by it will all be over in," he looked at his watch, "in eight hours."

They both walked back into the building together, Nate going back to churning, and Grant, completing the setting of the paper in the wrapping machine. Starting up the wrapper things went smooth; Leslie had lost interest and gone to the chicken coup to move, telepathically, items of interest, such as loose boxes and pieces of broken skids.

After the threshold of midnight had been crossed Grant realised, he needed boxes and another roll of wrap, so, he, after the machine had stopped, when the wrap had run out, went to the chicken coup to get it all together, not realising Nate was right behind him. Nate followed Grant into the chicken coup and, after Grant had thrown a stack onto the dolly, Nate grabbed Grant by the shoulders and abruptly kissed him on the mouth. Grant, in shock, took a few steps backwards tripping over the skid of boxes.

Falling onto his back, he slammed his head on the concrete floor and let out all his air. Confused and bewildered, angry and stunned his head in pain from encountering the rant passed out, the caretaker took this as the moment to cross over.

The caretaker, now possessing Grant got up and grabbing Nate, by the hair and began pulling Nate towards the production area in the direction of the readied butter in the far churn closest to the butter boat. Nate in an excited tone started bellowing, "Wait, waiiiiit, things went so well while you were out having a smoke, maybe I misunderstood when I was rubbing your shou…"

Grant, the caretaker, shoved Nate's head into the butter before he could finish his sentence and, holding it down, started counting.

Nate, arms flailing and legs pounding on the floor, was trying to grab anything to get out of the grasp of Grants grip but, the strength of the caretaker, the butter on the churn, and the anger of Grant made this impossible. Grant, now possessed by the caretaker, stopped counting at three hundred. In that time, Nate had stopped flailing and was motionless; then the caretaker crossed back to continue to observe, stood and watched Grant's reaction.

Grant, after letting go of Nate's hair, jumped back in horror, "What the fuck did I just do?" he questioned himself. "Holy fucking shit, what the fuck am I going to do?" he stood there staring in dismay and confusion. "What the fuck, what the fuck, what the fuck… Think, think, think, think, think?"

Looking around he realised that Nate was just getting ready to transfer the butter to the butter boat, and the butter tray was right there. This gave him a great idea, what he did is; leaving Nate where he was, Grant pushed the butter table over the top of Nate, hard, snapping his neck in the process, and went to the lunchroom, through the mixing area.

Sitting at the table, "What, what, what, what, what?" Getting up from the table, he got his phone from the dressing room and dialled 911.

Chapter 28

Sheryl showed up at the container, where Sam had performed his acts, knocking on the entrance, "In here and help me untie him. Sam insisted. The mixed feelings of disgust and terror overwhelmed her, and she stood frozen. She could never get used to seeing this, and tonight was more disgusting than she had ever witnessed; it's as though he knew something more than he was letting on.

Wrapping the body in the plastic roll he had, it is an eight-foot roll of dark plastic used for roofing strong and durable. They wrapped him and tuck taped it, tight, around him so no blood would drip or leak and dragged him to the car. Throwing him in the trunk, Sam glanced at the street and then down at Sheryl, "Follow me to the creamery, and we'll get this finished with," she agreed and got into her car and followed Sam to the plant.

They both went in, and Sam took her down to the room. It was in the basement of the creamery and way in the back where no one would suspect. Sam had jackhammered the slab and opened it to the dirt, already set with a three-foot by six-foot hole three feet deep.

"So you've dug this already; the last time, you had me dig it," she implied.

"Ya, well, I was in a good mood this week, and I had the energy to make it happen; anyway, let's go get him and finish this,"

Sam motioned her to the door and they both exited the room.

"Did you chip it out yourself?" she questioned.

"No, I got a temp to do it, one evening when I bring them in, nobody questions and nobody knows."

On the way out to the car, they saw something peculiar. Looking out from the office windows, they saw several police cruisers and a cube sitting in the parking lot, "I wonder what that's all about," Sheryl asked

He knew and said nothing. Going out to the parking lot, Sam asked boisterously, "What's going on here?"

"Up against the car and hands behind your back, both of you, NOW," came the demand of the police, as they were handcuffing the both of them.

"We've been watching you for months, ever since these suspicious deaths and events here have been happening, so many in the past few months are very abnormal so we've had you observed," Sam was put into the cube and Sheryl the cruiser and taken to the city lockup.

Chapter 29

When the police arrived Grant was standing outside, waiting to let them in. Leading them down to production, so they could observe the situation the police pulled Grant to the side so they could ask him some questions, just at that moment Sheryl walked in. Grant, while waiting for the police to arrive, had called her and told her to come down immediately there has been an incident and she needed to be here.

"What's going on?" she asked the first policeman she walked into.

"We're just trying to get that from your employee right now," the officer suggested.

"But I have a few questions to ask you as well," the officer implied. "There have been, over the course of a few months, some serious circumstances leading to very tragic situations, now I know that they have been deemed unfortunate accidents but I would like your statement on the events since they've been happening."

"I don't know what you're trying to imply, but I'm not going to answer anything unless my lawyer is present, so if you'll excuse me, I have some observations to make here, and I don't need you needling me on other topics that have been dealt with."

Sheryl in that moment of clarity pushed her way through to the churn in question to see Nate's disposition. When seeing him she broke down and fell to her knees, "how could this happen?"

The police left her alone, and while she was still kneeling on the floor, the EMS arrived and started taking pictures. It was such an unusual position they felt they needed pictures to help explain what they walked into.

After pronouncing him dead, they asked, "Is this a crime scene or can this body be removed?"

The medic standing over the body of Nate asked, "If we can remove him from here, we can get him to the coroners at the hospital now."

“We’re treating this as a crime scene right now so you’ll have to wait till the crime lab gets here to take pictures and observe the scene,” the officer directed.

“Okay, but if we get another call we’ll have to get out of here and come back when he’s ready to be transported.”

“No problem.”

The police had taken Grant to the lunchroom to question him, while the crime scene team looked over the body. It would be hours before they would move Nate and the EMS had left, being called on another call.

A crime scene detective then approached Sheryl and said, “I’ve noticed several cameras on the walls here. We would like to have the tapes so we can go over them to see what if anything is on them.”

“Yeah, sure, I’ll get them for you,” she left to get the tapes.

When handing them to the detective, she said, “I would like them back as soon as possible for our records as well.”

She handed them to him and went to her car to have a smoke.

Chapter 30

Grant was in the lunchroom with an officer answering questions relating to what had happened here and what he saw, "Where were you when the incident occurred?" the officer asked.

"I was right here in this room," Grant said answering the policeman.

"So I take it you didn't see anything then?"

"No."

"You know there are tapes that we've taken, and if they recorded anything, it will be on what happened here," the officer implied.

"Yes, but it's not going to show what you might suspect this is, cause it isn't what you're thinking, at least not by me," Grant argued.

Questions like these had gone on for three hours and everyone was tired and ready to go home and that's exactly what the officer did, "Well, we've gathered all we need at this time so I guess we're out of here you all have a better night see you, and you Grant, don't leave town."

"I've heard what you've said to the police. Is there anything you might want to add or say to me?" Sheryl questioned.

"No, I've said all there is on my end of things and I need to get out of here right now."

"I hear that," Sheryl agreed, they both got up. "Have a good night," they both said in unison.

"You don't have to come in tomorrow; stay home and take rest; after tonight, I would stay home for the rest of the week. They both left, and that's exactly what Grant did.

The police held onto the tapes for six weeks when they were returned to Sheryl, she was told that there was nothing on them and that the machine had either been turned off or faulty. All they could do is go by the crime scene itself and photos. The guy, that was here, had nothing he could add so he told her they would be in touch if anything resulted from the evidence.

Leslie had, during the attack, done something insightful; he had tampered with the video machine just as the situation was occurring in the chicken coup. Witnessing the crossing over, he, Leslie, darted to the office where the video was set up and turned off the recorder the video machine was still running, so it didn't look as though it was tampered with, it just wasn't recording anything. He knew something was going to happen that should not be recorded, and he liked Grant, so he made sure nothing, of the event that was about to happen, was recorded. When Sheryl was handed back the tapes, she put them in to see what she might find and it was just as the police said nothing.

A few months later the creamery was sent a report about the incident and the autopsy showed that, though there was bruising on the back of Nate's head it wasn't done with a force of malicious intent. During the investigation it was discovered that the floors were uneven and it is believed that as Nate was bent over, reaching in to do whatever it is he does before transferring the butter, the butter boat started rolling and caught him off guard, pinning him in the butter, face down and as he tried to free himself he snapped his neck, freakishly, on the butter table and fell, face first into the butter, paralysed, and suffocated. It was deemed an accident, a weird unfortunate accident.

Sheryl made it a point to tell Grant this so he could relax and get past the whole experience of that night, all Grant could do is grin; he had gotten away with murder. That night went smooth as butter, with no problems and no tragedies.

Chapter 31

While the department was doing their investigation of the creamery, as a crime scene, it would be shut down for at least five days, depending on what was found, maybe longer if they found anything that would need further investigation. They had been digging in the basement of the creamery for at least four days and discovered three bodies.

For the short time, they had been here; it was quite unexpected. Plus, the one found in the back of the car that made four.

The creamery had only been there, about, two years and the findings here brought the owner into the question of being more. The building they had moved from was still uninhabited so going in, to do an inspection and perhaps bring it into the investigation as well wouldn't be an issue to the owner. It was still owned by Sam; no one had bought or leased it so it was taped off and a team of cadaver dogs was put together to start sniffing around.

There were two teams one for the exterior the other for the basement, they were in the basement for thirty minutes before the dogs began to get really excited, that's when they brought in the heavy equipment, to start chipping the floor of the old building. The dogs on the exterior also became excited on the asphalt of the parking lot, again, heavy equipment would have to be brought in, to do the digging of the hardened surface.

"These dogs are going nuts," one of the officers said.

"And it's not just in one place they seem to be all over the lot and the basement has the same reaction from the other team."

"Well, then I guess we have our work cut out for us over the next few months as we go over the grounds here. We don't know how many or how big the area is and from the observation of the dogs it's very big," the lead detective implied.

It was the end of March, and though the weather was starting to warm, it was cold and blustery. The snow was beginning to fall and they decided to call it off till it got warmer over the next few days, the ground would be easier and it would be more pleasant. The chipping in the basement could start immediately, so, as they did it became apparent that there was a difference in the colour of the concrete some areas were lighter than others.

“Look for areas like this one this place is large but not undiscoverable. If you see an area like this, it means it’s been changed, a lot newer than what it is supposed to be,” said the captain.

As they were walking the basement the captain got on the phone to the other two teams at the creamery, “We have discovered a difference of colour with the concrete in the basement here, that’s what you should be looking for, there, as well.”

“Okay,” answered the team at second sight. The digging at the first sight only lasted a week there were only three bodies to be discovered, but the second sight was different. There were several patches with the asphalt that were dug up and several bodies found in each ten in all around the parking lot. But the basement was a different kind.

The basement of the old sight had at least twenty spots that were being chipped and dug so it was taking a very long time to, first, find them, then to chip each one. The walls became an area of question, as well, so they were also checked, but came up empty.

Sam, during this time, kept his promise and pleaded guilty to all charges and took total accountability letting the courts know that Sherryl was coerced into helping him dispose and cover up each incident and that she is an unwilling participant.

Sherryl, after the interrogation and investigation, settled into her new position and began a new sense of herself in the world of Ice cream and butter. Still I, the caretaker, am watching.

Characters:

Brent: Main, new guy
Celina: Brent’s girlfriend
Nate: Mixer/churn operator/pasteuriser/ice cream maker
Craig: Daytime churn operator
Sherryl: Manager
Sam: Owner
Stan: Evening churn operator

Austin: Evening crew with Brent wrapping operator
Jerry: Daytime wrapping operator/soon to be the mixer
Dan: Maintenance guy
Brenda: Lab tech
Grant: Switched to production from shipping
Karen: Shipping manager
Ingrid: Yoghurt production Cliff: Day timer wrapper

Muse

One hundred malicious little mysteries
Ends up in some bodies fantasies
Someone else to recognise
Yet, in the end it's based on lies

One hundred malicious little mysteries
Have entered into my midnight sleep
Reflecting back it cannot be
Still I can't escape the dream

One hundred malicious little mysteries
Have entered into your midnight sleep
Reflecting back to recognise
And still it comes out based on lies

Schynstyk Park
Prologue

This is a grouping of stories that have come from the depth of sleep. They are the essence of nightmares and though there are more I thought I would start with these and then present the others at a later time some in a novel form and others will be as well short stories.

Depicted in a rural park setting these poltergeists, ghosts, in life, were rapists, killers and stalkers that now roam the park in search of victims and pray on the week and depressed. They haunted me in dreams for many years so I thought I would share them in the hopes that they would be released from my mind and be given new minds to invade.

Story 1
The Brook

I am a wanderer I can move between all the grounds; most have limited access to one or two, but I have the choice of any and right now I chose here, at the parking lot entrance. I can see the grassy hill from the boarding forested lake, but I chose to be closer so here at the bench I wait for the happening. We are all waiting for it.

Tonight, there are ten in the dark; they cannot be seen as the party arrived, by van, with a new load. This was a common occurrence, every three or four months, on a good year. The days are irregular so the chance to miss a happening is a possibility if I am in another area of the park.

Some lurk behind bushes, and others behind trees, one or two like to remain in the open. I myself like the bench, to watch from, once in a while to sit or lay, but this time I'm hiding with one of the stuck one's. We watched as the van made its way down the dirt road, about a mile into the park.

Getting out of the van and walking to the back to unlock the trailer doors the driver looked around to see if anyone was watching.

"We have to be careful," he said. "We don't want anyone to be around, there are predators in these wooded areas and, If anyone saw, it wouldn't go down right."

Unlocking the doors, he swung them open and looked inside; his swamper stood beside him; and they both smiled.

"Get them out of the van and unchain them," he said busying himself with the keys and throwing them at the second.

"Ya, man" he answered back catching them and jumped up into the trailer.

He motioned them to jump down and began unlocking the chains, where the driver was standing. There were five women all scantily dressed in bras and panties, with their hands chained behind their backs and ankle bracelets as well.

They all had a hard look, as though they had not been cleaned for days and showed signs of malnourishment.

"They isss beautiful issss they notssss," he asked in his snake-like hiss, "my preferencccce issss the brunettsssseesssss," the stuck one said, exaggerating his slur wherever he can.

"Yes, they are, but I prefer the blonds the longer the hair the better, there is so much that can be done with long hair," I said with a smirk.

"Dosssssse you think there will be enough to playsssss with, the lassssst load only hadsssss one, and there wassssss at leassssst eight in the fieldssssss, she wassssssss gone in lessssss time it takessssss to peelssss a banana," he said looking at his hands.

"Oooo, theysss coming out," as they jumped down off of the back end they gathered around the side on the grass and huddled together to try to keep warm.

Some of them looked into the park, and, it appeared as though they were looking right at us but that is impossible, after all, we are dead and trapped here for eternity.

It has been six months since the last drop and, in their excitement, two are standing right in front of the van, just a few yards away, not caring if they are observed or felt. These predators are the first to strike, Sex perverts, assailants, and rapists that are mostly into terrifying the innocents and the unaware, the more aggressive usually hang back until the van leaves and there are only the victims left, standing or sitting.

Not all of us are aware of not being seen; the rapists want to be known and are usually standing right in front of their selected victim. They will walk upon them and touch their hair or grab them around the neck, the buttocks, or, what they refer to as the cherry sweet spots. There are only three here today, and that's because they are stuck here, so they are always here and always the first to act. It goes in an order of act assault.

The sexual and violent assaults go first, they aren't killers but they are highly sexed and can go on for hours and the longer the better. Most of the time they will attack from behind and two on one will be with the victim when there are only one or two objects. That means all holes are entered, but on a night like tonight, they will have everyone for a period of time in order to give each one their personal best, and move onto the next in sight. When the first of the line-up of predators are done with their subjects that's when the torture begins, from the more severe entities, and none, of the victims, are spared.

When there are many victims, then there is tonight, to apprehend, it's hard to entertain them all, in turn, and some end up escaping. This is not a good thing, it leaves too many questions to be answered and the police are in the area for months. This brings everything to a halt and all there is the endurance of time and patience. It makes the whole area a vortex of negative energy and we won't see the truck or van, sometimes, for a year or two.

Tonight, though, some have fled to the forested area, the more violent apparitions are there lurking in the forest waiting for them.

This gives them the opportunity to get their cravings satisfied before they are molested by the first wave of poltergeist, keeping these targets fresh, so to speak. All the subjects brought here are from the streets, hookers, drug addicts, as well, people who have crossed the crime bosses by snitching or owing large amounts of money. Yes, sometimes there are men standing out there grouped in with the hoard of victims, it's not always women, as it is tonight, there are no men.

Tonight we have ten of us for five of them, this is good. The rapists and violent assaults started as soon as the van left the parking lot. I'm sure when looking back and seeing the ones, they left convulsing or running into the park, the two, in the van. Only thing that it's from the cold or drug-induced fear of being in the park so late and what might be waiting for them. We are unseen, and the two, in the truck, delivering the goods, have only been told to drop off the girls and ignore what is witnessed.

In actuality, the girls are being molested by the first phase of the night. Raped and battered, thrown and beaten into delirium or, unconsciousness. Two or three try to flee but, without success, there are the stockers on the outer limits tonight and none can get past them.

They can be the most violent of all, they cover all grounds, and I don't mean territory, I mean sexual assault, battery, torture, and finally killing. They are the scariest of us, most of us have one thing or two things that give us the thrill and excitement we crave but, they are everything in one force of terror.

One of the blonds was crawling to a bench after the first assault, and I knew when I first saw her that she would be my first tonight. There were only two I wanted, and I was hoping she would be one of the first attacked, and she was.

When he was done with her, I started on my speciality biting and strapping. She was already tied and tired from the ghostly violent sex; the blood was oozing from her mouth and anus; and there were deep gouges on her breasts.

I enjoy licking the blood as it oozes from the open wounds; we are poltergeists and can interact, when the terror and horror are high and fanatical, with the living, as though we are a part of their being.

I have her by the hair and drag her across the grounds, a third, from the forested area, chases us down to begin his methods of abuse.

"She's mine, she's mine," he screamed as he grabbed her neck. "You pulled out some strands," he said. "She's bleeding. I like that; you've set her up nicely."

I like to fuel the fever of the goon; it makes things happen at a more dramatic and faster pace. I don't like to kill, that is not my passion or skill, I leave that up to the menacing of the deranged. These are the ones who kill for sport and the thrill of watching the life drain from the victim.

Myself, I like to orgasm on her while there is blood all over her body, I drop her and let the one who is chasing us do his thing. As I grab a hold of my next pretty, I watch, I like to do that sometimes as well. He begins by licking her face; this is common practice with most of us. It's like a smell, it captures the moment, and lets the victim know there is no way out, and he has her and shows no remorse.

"Ah, my sweet thing you thought you were going to escape. I've waited eight months for you, the last truck was a wash there was only one and she was gone in a few moments after she arrived. No endurance."

We have no weapons and rely on the ability to manipulate solids in the physical world with our mind and body, so he begins to choke, and hold her down while he is sucking the breath out of her. I cannot watch, and avert my attention to my next assault, and she is beautiful.

"Don't struggle I gritted," they cannot hear us but feel every intense strike we deliver. We can get inside their heads but then we have to enter their bodies to do that and that diminishes the time we have to spend.

The previous attacker was modest with his assault, because there are more ghosts than expected this time, and this one will satisfy me for the remainder of the night. With care, I bite her neck so as to only draw small blood flow. As a ghoul or phantom, all fluids are tasteless, so I rely on my memory, which makes this interaction more responsive and enjoyable.

"Ahhh, the memories it brings, can you hear me."

I yelled in her ear. "Can you see me?" I again yelled into her ear.

After I have entered her mouth and button and the moments with her were beautiful, it must have been hours, but was only felt like a few moments in time;

we cannot orgasm, but we know they feel us. She was all contorted and dirty, the way I like to leave them. When I finished, I dragged her to the bushes where another is waiting and leave her to him.

He is a finaliser after he's finished, she will be killed as his final act. The amazing thing is the soulless parasites wait their turn, in order of assault, so the torture is in the sequence of extreme, and death is the final realisation for each victim.

As I walk through the brook borough, looking around, there is no one in sight. Even with as many pretties to use tonight, there was still time to dispose of all the victims and make each one disappears. People wonder why shallow graves are dug, it's a matter of time, even with one or two there is so much activity that it goes on for most of the night and hiding, even one corpse becomes an effort against time.

My time here is finished and was most enjoyable, but there is another place that I love to wait at, and I have waited there going on three years for the right victim. While I was there the last time, I overheard a couple talking about visitors from out of state that were interested in seeing the park for the first time and planned on bringing them in the spring.

Story 2
The Pond

I am at my favourite place in this location, and I wait impatiently for the visitors. It is the beginning of spring, but waiting doesn't mean it can or will happen at any moment. What it means is, it can and will happen in spring but, the years can pass quickly, and I can be here for a millennium of time without knowing. But that is not the case it has only been five years, waiting for the visitors.

But are they the right visitors? I watch to see and know when they refer to the time before, and how beautiful it was then as now. She is blond with red high lights, which only arouses me more. Her partner has left her on her own and says he'll be back in a few hours. She smiles and waves.

"Are you going to be alright on your own?" he said loudly as he was standing a few hundred yards away, his voice echoing in the air off the cliffs behind her.

"Yes," she said smiling; her teeth were so white and perfect. "Go; I'll be waiting here when you return."

I watched as he got in the car and drove off. When I was in the world of solids, that's how I refer to them that way there's no real attachment, I was a peeper and a stocker before I went on the attack. That way I knew who I was dealing with, how much time I had during each playful moment, and whom to expect if ever there was an interruption.

That's what I was doing with this one; it makes the moment of attack more exciting and heightens the arousal so that the time spent in the game is more sensual and expressive and I know she feels it too.

I have different senses of sensitivities in each area, in this area I can make the player not just feel me but hear me as well. This allows for a more explicit understanding for her and gives me the opportunity to say, in advance, what she is going to look forward to in our most intimate moments before they are experienced. But for now, I watch.

Walking up to her, I whisper into the wind, "Hey."

She is startled. She turns and faces me, as though I'm being seen but I'm a ghost. All she sees is the whirling dust funnel entwined with leaves.

I whisper again this time; it's her name, "Sarah."

Again, she is shaken. I brush her hair with my fingers; she can feel this, but it always comes across as the wind. She is still startled and swipes at the air as though to stop me, but she touches nothing.

I whisper her name again in conjunction with the breeze as it wisps her hair across her face. Her face contorts, and she goes into a moment of distracted fear. Her lip begins to quiver, and I see a bead of sweat on her forehead.

She, and her man, set up their picnic halfway through this section of the park where the trees are hanging low, the weeping willows are many here, and it's easy to lose yourself in them. She begins to run, starting at a quick pace, towards the parking lot, but I can see she is disoriented and headed north instead of east, right into my favourite part of the park.

Where the willow I call grandfather stands, it is the oldest and mostly full of weeping branches that hang over the pond in a thick bundle, overlooking the pond, and is the most beautiful. Set right next to a small creek that flows into it she walks right into the middle of the hanging branches, where, if you aren't looking for anyone or anything you wouldn't see what is beneath the branches.

That's why it's my favourite. I grab her hair and throw her against the trunk, whispering, "Isn't this fun, Sarah?"

I whisper in her ear. She tries to scream, but the breeze is too heavy and squelches it in the branches.

"What do you think of the weather now," I whisper, as she tightens her back to the tree and slides down the trunk to a seated position.

She searches in her purse and pulls out her cell phone, and called her husband.

"Honey, there is something terribly wrong here. I'm frightened by whatever it is, and I need to leave ASAP."

She cuts the call and stands. Getting her barring, she realises she was headed in the wrong direction and starts on her way to the parking lot. But she doesn't know I'm watching and walking beside her and behind her.

Until "Sarahhhhhhhhh" is whispered again into the wind as her hair wisps around her face. I trip her with some tumbleweed as it blows by.

"Fucking bullshit," she screamed barely making a sound into the torrent of the wind. Not just a gentle breeze now, a storm is starting to blow and the sky is beginning to look dangerously vicious. The weather here changes very quickly, and when conditions are right, oh so right, like now, well?

"I didn't realise I'd come so far, time and distance got away from me in the heat of the day," she said allowed. Talking to herself always seemed to calm her when she felt fear or insecure or unsure of herself in situations like this.

Looking into the distance, she could see the parking lot but she couldn't have walked that kind of distance in the short time she had been there, could she? She thought to herself the run had taken her further than she realised.

Continuing walking she began to realise that though she was walking forward, towards the parking lot, the landscape was moving backwards, as though the wind were blowing her back from where she came, to the grandfather of all weeping willows, my domain.

What was really happening is I'd lifted her and began manipulating the ground beneath her. She still felt like she was on the ground when in actual fact she is floating, mesmerised by the landscape and the changing weather. It has a hypnotic effect on some people especially when they are feeling overwhelmed by panic. And she is back in my domain.

Grabbing her again by the hair with my other hand, I pull off her blows. Surprisingly, her bra is removed by the blustering wind. I bite her on the mouth, and she begins to bleed; this is all done in gusts of wind, and it all appears to be happening in correlation to the storm. Freaky, her pants give the impression to just fly off with another gust.

She screams but can't be heard above the clasping sound of thunder. She is half-naked, and it seems as though it were storm related until I put my head between her cheeks, and my tongue enters her button and her vagina. She is beautiful. My hands begin to caress her breasts and thighs and my fingers enter her mouth.

She, surprising to me, begins sucking on them. I think she knows and is playing along. Or is feeling amorous in the moment and believing it to be a dream. Anyway, she is going with the whole act and appears to be enjoying it.

So after toying with her, with my tongue, I enter her button with her on all fours. We are still inside the willow, and the torrent of wind has calmed. She is not screaming now but moaning with pleasure, this is something I have never experienced in the one hundred years of being.

She turns to her back and starts fondling her clitoris. She begins moaning louder and it seemed as though there were a bonding of souls at that moment together. This was so new to me, not knowing what to do, I let her leave. She found what clothes she could and put them on.

Going back to the parking lot, she found her husband, he had only just arrived moments before she got there; I never saw them or her ever again. I was lost for a half-century after that. She had vexed me with her spell of desire. I just ended up wandering the park watching, nothing interested me except her possible return.

Story 3
The Netting

He stood on the edge of the path where the stone bridge stood over the brook and the walking path meet with the lake. He climbed on top of the rail and looked over the surface of the lake, then brought his eyes beneath him and looking into the brook and focusing on the bottom he saw a twinkling of light. It was early evening and the sun was glimmering over the lake at an angle that made the surface look like a mirror, but losing right below him, he could see clear to the bottom with little or no effort.

The twinkling aroused his curiosity and he decided, at that moment, he would challenge the current to find out what the glimmering in the water is. Climbing down from the stone rail he undressed to his under ware and walked to the area where he saw the shining flicker beneath the bridge.

He started to wade into the brook, the cold of the water made his body shiver and his hairs stand on end, in the place where he thought he would be closest he began to realise the depth of the area and turned around got out and got dressed.

He thought to himself, "I'll just come back in a few days with some diving equipment and do some spot checking."

It had been more than a few days before his return, having to buy what he needed and not knowing anything about diving, he first purchased a snorkel and some fins. As he thought about the depth, he began to think that the snorkel will help him to discover what it is and its location but wouldn't give enough time to do any digging or the ability to stay at the bottom for any length of time.

So, going back to the sporting goods store, he purchased an air tank, weights, wrist weights, a belt and a camera. He had discovered that the rocky bed was slippery and has a lot of sharp edges due to the layers of bedrock.

As he was preparing for the first dive, he thought he saw someone standing on the other side of the brook but on second look there was no one there and he dismissed it as his imagination going skew In his excitement for discovery. He had taken a one-day course to familiarise himself with the diving equipment and found it enough to put him into the mode of the moment. He believed he was smart enough to know how to handle the turbulence of the water and didn't think it didn't require much skill, after all the depth was maybe ten or fifteen feet what could possibly go wrong.

The few times, he was out snorkelling gave him a good understanding and he had done some scuba diving during a holiday off the Florida Keys in 2011.

How much different could this be?

Not taking into account his physical situation, suffering from asthma and arrhythmia, his decision was, still, to do this alone. His curiosity and greed getting in the way of responsible consideration, to the prospect of something valuable, of the feat he is about to undertake.

As he waded out to his waist, he remembered that he hadn't checked his air or turned on the tanks. He is wearing two, for the maximum time, he will be fighting a current, which can make the situation difficult, and would take up a lot of time anchoring himself in one position. As he reached over his head to his back, where the valve is to turn on his air, he glanced across the brook and saw again a small figure observing what he was doing. He looked down at the area he was about to dive into and then took a second look to see if there was really someone watching and saw no one.

Dismissing it as a hallucination he plunged into the brook and began his descent to where he assumed the glimmer of the thing would be. Even with the weights around his waist, he found that the current was pulling him with it and away from the object and had to grab rocks to force himself to the location.

Finding the rock was not as easy as he thought it would be, and realising, everything looked different when observed from the shoreline. It took twenty-five minutes to find the right area and another twenty to find the rock but when he did what he saw excited him to the core.

The current wasn't as strong in the place he was but still felt that anchoring himself to something would make it easier to keep him in one place. That took another thirty minutes. He tried moving the rock covering the netting but it was buried deep and turned out to be larger than expected. He began removing the surrounding bedrock, as that was his only alternative, and realised, he had already been down three hours and he was on his second tank.

There was more rock than sand and even though it was removed easily exposing the netting was difficult, but he was able to and as the netting began to reveal itself, he saw what was glimmering from the crossing. His eyes became wide with excitement as he started to uncover what looked like a chest. The removal of the bedrock took a major amount of time and in his eagerness, he lost track of it and that's when things started to go very wrong.

He had anchored himself to, what he thought was, a deep routed tree branch but with his erratic movements and excitement, the branch had started to come loose. Unobserved by him he continued to remove rocks and debris causing the branch to become more and more displaced. When he noticing what looked like a keyhole to what might be a lock, he felt his elation rise to extreme anticipation and that's when it began to happen.

Glancing up to the surface he thought he saw, again, a figure hovering above him but again dismissed it as a deviation, his mind just playing tricks and went back to removing the rocky bed. Forgetting to check his air supply, at the time his prize began to reveal itself, he started to notice tightness in his chest, that's when he decided to check his air and realised that both tanks are empty. But that wasn't what was causing the chest tightness, it was his heart. In his excitement, his blood pressure began to rise and his heart began to beat faster putting a major strain on him and he began to panic.

Depleted of his air, he franticly started towards the surface without realising what he had done at the beginning of his dig. Anchored to a branch, which is enrooted in the bedrock, he did his best to be freed from its snare but only ended up pulling it from the bottom. The branch is a large size, almost a log, but not the trunk of a tree, and it had been submerged for so long that its buoyancy was compromised and though it could float, due to the current, it remained submerged, barely skimming the surface.

By the time he realised what he had done it was too late. He felt a very strong tug and the branch began dragging him down towards the lake. The first tug sent him to the bottom of the brook out of control and his air, depleted, was causing him to convulse he tried to grab anything on the bottom to stop himself, but the branch was too heavy and he was too week, from lack of air and the onset of a heart attack. He was not able to maintain a firm grip on anything, not like there was anything to grab. As he was beginning to resurface, he again found himself trapped by the branch. Where he had tied off, which caused him to be underneath the branch, as it headed towards the lake.

Trapping him below the surface, making it impossible for him to catch a breath, his air gone and as the branch entered the lake, its speed slowed to almost a stop, he tried one last flip of his flippers. At that moment he realised that they had been ripped off his feet, during the struggle, and he went nowhere. Entangled in the tether, he would have found it nearly impossible to free himself even if he had lived through the turbulence of the brook. He couldn't even think about his next move as he entered the lake because life had completely escaped him right at that moment.

Adrift in the middle of the lake, he could not be seen, trapped under the branch submerged and lifeless. He was not found for a week, even though there were several search parties out looking for him. It wasn't until the branch had floated to the shoreline that he was discovered.

Story 4
Koreg

September 15

It started with an ex-con, While sitting in a kitchen drinking, talk was off the cuff remarks about relationships and toughing it out while inside. Koreg can't resist smug comments, like the one he delivered, "If it were up to me anyone stuck behind bars gets what they deserve, If a guard wants them, rape is only part of the sentence, and they should know they are there for the enjoyment of whoever wants their time."

"How, can you say something like that, have you ever been inside?" She asked with an insulted tone. "Or are you just mouthing off because you think it's funny?" She said with rage, her grimacing look and squinted eyes.

"No, but I haven't done anything stupid enough to put me there, that's why I'm free and the idiots behind the walls aren't," he said with a drunken smirk and a sarcastic tone.

That's when she flew across the table and, grabbing him by the throat, threw him to the ground. They both landed hard, with her on top, she, for her size, is quite agile and got up using Korey as a prop. She began kicking him in the face and chest then everything went black for him.

Coming to his senses on the grass, on the front lawn, he realised that he must have been dragged outside. Discovering he is bleeding from his mouth he got up and tried to brush himself off. Staggering, he bumped into a tree and put out his hand to hold himself up against it.

Wiping his face off, he started to take his first steps, and thought to himself, "*What?*" he tried taking a few steps and fell, "Fuck" came flying from his lips, "Fucking ice," he said allowed then thought, "*I feel like I'm taking my first steps,*" he spit out a blood smirking snicker and did his best to get to his feet.

Getting to the park Koreg began crossing the field, as he reached midway, he stepped into a semi-deep hole and fell again. Realising his shoe had come off he began digging around for it, getting himself soaked in the process. Finding his shoe he was on his way again.

Getting himself to the front door he fishes his pockets for the key, "FUCK," he yells "*I must have lost it when I fell in the park*," he thought and then feels around for his glasses, "*FUCK, I lost them too*."

He starts tapping on windows, finding no one home he decided to go to the store to buy smokes and when going to pay for it he discovered she had stolen his money while he was lying unconscious outside, so, he walked back home. After an hour his roommate comes walking up the walkway to the front door, from the car that had just dropped him off. "What's the problem Korr?" he asked.

"I lost my fucking keys and I can't get in," he blithered, spitting blood mixed saliva, at his roommate.

"Wow, you're looking in rough shape; good thing, I came home when I did you might have frozen to death."

"Ya."

They both went in and relaxed with a beer.

September 22

The next two weeks went smooth, this gave Koreg time to heal from his wounds and prepare for the coming events. He had met a girl and was excited about having been single for ten months previous. In his glorified crass best he said, "Ya, man I'm finally getting my dicky sticky so my moods at work here are going to be better," and they were, even after this next encounter.

While he was taking the garbage out his girlfriend came home with some friends, who all happen to be men, she had met at the mall. She didn't tell him they were ex-boyfriends, and just as he got in the door, bam, he got punched in the face.

"Hey…" he tried to say but then got pushed down the stairs and onto his back.

"What the hell…" is all he got out before being stomped on the stomach. He scrambled to his feet and went into the living area just as he was tackled to the floor over the couch. They wrestled on the floor for a moment, then, Koreg managed to pull himself free.

Popping up to greet another ex – standing over him he was tripped into the clothing space, beside the entrance door. The next one then jumped on top of him and started kneeing Koreg. Not realising that Koreg's foot was twisted in a way, caught by the closet sliding door, the weight of the ex - snapped Koreg's ankle and the kneeing to his chest fractured several ribs.

This action inspired the girlfriend to react and send the exes out of the residence and Koreg was able to find his footing and sit down to relax and call a cab to make his way to the hospital, where he was bandaged and cast after the resetting of his foot, which had been twisted out of shape. He was then told he would be off work for the next five weeks.

November 30

After returning to work, he began to settle into his job. After a week he started to talk about how good it is again, between him and his girlfriend, and how he is looking forward to the Christmas holiday. The next week was different; he came to work wearing sunglasses. When he removed them, he had two black eyes. He then started to explain how, through the weekend, he and his girlfriend, roommate, had broken up and after going out for a few hours he came back to find his "roommate" with a guy she had just met, at the corner store, in his bed fucking. After throwing the stranger out, they argued about it for a few hours. Settling down they decided to prepare some food and watch TV.

During the food preparation the roommate's girlfriend came over and they started drinking. The girlfriend took an interest in Koreg while he was eating, and began making advances towards him, knowing what had just happened previously. This made the roommate very jealous. Seeing this Koreg and the girlfriend left and went to her house where they engaged in their own sexual excitement over the next few hours. Koreg then went home and went to bed.

While he was asleep his roommate came into his room and started hitting him with a broom handle, and fists. Waking up to this violent attack he grabbed for the stick and forcibly ripped it from her hands. Seeing that he was bleeding and feeling the pain, in a fit of rage, he began punching her and threw her up against the living room wall. Holding her by the throat he started to choke her.

"How do you like it?" he screamed. "Does it feel good to be going through this?"

She couldn't respond, and she was so traumatised. She just went limp and passed out. Koreg dropped her to the floor and began making a cup of coffee.

December 6

Still just living as roommates they began engaging in three-way sex relations with another girl they had moved in. Koreg came to work with some terrific stories of long nights of sex, drugs and drinking. He then began hinting about how his roommate didn't like sharing him with the new partner and her jealousy was getting in the way of a great thing.

The next week, as we were working, he told me he had found a new place to live and needed help moving. I agreed to help if he would buy gas and give some money for my time. Agreeing to my request it was planned for the Friday of that same week.

After moving him into the new place things went smooth for two months. One day, after the holidays, he came to work with a fat lip. Koreg then began to explain how controlling his new roommate is, that he couldn't have friends over, or his ex-roommate, girlfriend, and had to have permission to have anyone in the house. So, he needed to move out again and asked if I could help him do that at the end of the month, reluctantly, I agreed.

While we were moving his stuff out there was an argument about the wrongness of this move and that he can't just jump out without paying rent for next month. After being slapped around, for an hour, they both came to the conclusion that it is the best thing because it could only get worse from here on.

After finishing moving Koreg back to his old residence, with his roommate, girlfriend. Weeks later he told me how he was with his roommate, sexually again, and her friend came in to visit and drink. That's when it started getting interesting. The friend, who just got there, started feeling the alcohol and hitting on Koreg.

As they were kissing, Koreg said to her "You understand when I came in here it was to be just friends," reminding her that they can be with whomever they want. "And, besides, you were just with your ex so all's fair in love and war," Koreg added.

So she joined them, for a more exclusive performance. That's when koreg and the girlfriend got up and left the house. Not trying to make her jealous, no! Not trying to provoke anything no, and he went to the friend's house to be together, alone.

When he got back she had visitors, just a few friends and family over for a party. As he sat down to join them they offered him a beer. Reaching out to grab it, bam.

“Hey, what was that for,” Koreg demanded.

“You think just cause you to know us you can have what we offer for free.”

“You were handing it to me.”Koreg implied.

“Where did you just come from?” They demanded.

“A friend’s.”

“Her, girlfriend.”

“So, ya,” Koreg replied.

That’s when he got slammed in the back of the head with a beer. Getting up off the floor “What the fuck” he said looking at his roommate. Putting on his hoody and jacket he started up the stairs to the front door. Just as he was cresting the top stair he was grabbed by his hood and pulled back. The staircase was of a different design it had five stairs to the right of the front door then a small landing that turned on a forty-five-degree angle and down another six stairs to a door entrance into the basement suite.

Falling onto the landing in a clump all that came out was “Shit” just before he got kicked in the ribs, there’s a five-foot space between the door threshold and stairs and the force of the kick was so great he flew through the door and landed three feet into the living room.

“What, you don’t want me to leave?”

“No,” she said with a snide grin. “I know you have no place to go, and you would be headed back to that bitch so you’re staying here.”

“And, what if I don’t want to.”

“Then before you leave, you’ll be beaten even more and you don’t want that do you.”

“No.”

She popped open a beer and handed it to him and told him to sit on the sofa.

December 19

Arriving at work I looked at him and he had his jaw in a wired mesh.

“What happened?” I enquired.

“I’ll tell you during the break,” he said through the wire.

The whole time working I couldn’t help but not think of ways he would have been beaten to end up in that state. So during the break, he began.

“I was sleeping, and out of nowhere ‘BAM’ I woke up, surprised, and rolled off the other side of the bed and landed on the floor. There she was standing over me with a pot ready to hit me again. I quickly got up and she swung. I grabbed her arm with my left hand and swung with my right hitting her in the side of the head.

Grabbing her by the hair I threw her on the bed and hit her a few more times, with the pot and my fist, in the back of the head. Then I pulled her off and threw her into the living room and slammed the door shut putting a chair under the door handle to hold it shut. I went back to sleep getting up to an empty house I went out to have a few beers.

When I returned that's when the shit started. She had a person, in my room, and they were fucking on my bed. I grabbed the guy by the hair and threw him into the living room and told him to leave. "This is my place and I pay to be here and I want you out."

The guy got dressed fast and left. I asked her who that guy was, and she said, "I met him on the street. I had known him from a few years before so, I asked him in for a coffee. After talking for a while we began fucking and that's when you walked in," she explained self-righteously.

Koreg started shaking his head, "That was a few days ago, I didn't know it at the time but her boyfriend, who was in jail, was getting out and she had a plan."

We both started eating sandwiches, and he continued, "After we got off work, the past weekend, I met her in the mall. We were just standing there talking and from out of nowhere, BAM. Her boyfriend suckered me from behind. I thought we were friends and what it turned out to be is, they were both setting me up for this. It did feel a little suspicious when she wanted to meet me after work, but I went anyway. I'll tell you the rest later." The break was over, and we went back to it. Later that night we finished early and while relaxing in the changing room he continued, "She wanted it to happen at the mall, cause the security guards would be there to break it up. I was bleeding so badly the security called an ambulance and took me to the hospital. I just got out six hours ago with this. He hit me so hard he knocked out two teeth and broke my jaw. So, they had to wire it back into place. I still have to go back for surgeries after this comes off." Koreg explained.

"Holy fuck," I said in amazement, "And you're still living with her?" I enquired.

"Ya."

"Why? She's going to get you killed eventually you know. At least it seems as though she's setting you up to be killed. You need to get out and let her live on her own she's someone that can't live with anyone. You as well, you need to live on your own."

"I can't. I love her and she has been hurt so many times you know Dana used to beat her up every day," he said sipping on his energy drink.

"Ya, I wonder why?" I replied. Then he said, "The more you tell me to leave her the more I want her."

I couldn't believe he just said that, it was as though he wanted to live this nightmare like he deserved it, as a punishment for leaving his wife and son.

"Okay," I said bewildered and left it at that.

January 5

It was smooth through the holidays I guess they have respect for each other at that time and remained somewhat peaceful. There were a few scuffs but nothing major. It wasn't until this one morning right after work he had just walked in the door and she laid in on him about leaving the counter a mess before going to work.

She started hitting him and he reminded her that if she ever started anything again, he was going to make sure she regretted it. He had had enough and wouldn't hold back. So, as she swung, he ducked, he then threw her up against the wall, pushing it in with her body, not breaking it, but leaving a crease in it with the shape of her.

He stepped back and punched her square in the temple knocking her to the floor, then hit her again in the jaw, breaking it and knocking out two of her front teeth. That's when it ended, they called an ambulance, rushed her to the hospital where she was then wired up and sent home after two days. He came to work bragging about that one and said that he warned her, she didn't believe him until it happened.

February 13

Koreg is preparing something special for his roommate. She has never been to fine dining restaurants, one can only imagine why, so he thought he would do something that she would remember. It would take place at the tower he has the ring and bought a suit and made sure it was a late one, a 10 o'clock dinner that way they could have drinks before and after, to celebrate if things went well.

They spent that afternoon drinking hard and as the limo pulled up, she started puking all over the lawn and herself. Going back in to change she exclaimed, "It was the idea of taking such an expensive ride she was nervous," she lied.

When she returned, she was dressed casually, in jeans and a loose white blouse, she didn't shower so she still had the smell of vomit on her with a dusting of perfume to try to cover it up. She got into the limo and they were on their way. On the way there, they did a few more lines of cocaine and she went down on him. Even with the mixture of bile and perfume he still felt overwhelmed with excitement and exploded into her mouth.

Getting out of the limo, in front of the tower, they looked very off-set clashing with incoordination of clothing and dishevelled, after the orgasmic ride there. She, not realising her state, started into the foyer and headed to the elevator. When she was stopped by security. "Hey, were do you think youre going?" he asked with a stern tone. She replied, "We have a reservation in the tower," and tried to continue but was overwhelmed by two more guards, "Not like that you don't," and they began to escort her out.

Koreg was startled by this and asked what was wrong but before he could get an answer, he was jumped from behind and tackled to the ground. Both were put in handcuffs and taken to the holding room.

"What's going on," Koreg asked when the officer entered the room.

"We have suspicions about your girlfriend, it appears she is wanted for several violations and obstructions and was recognised when entering the lobby."

"Oh."

"You're okay to leave but she's going downtown to be arraigned." The night was over, before it even began.

"Koreg was left in the lobby, alone, wondering what he should do. Then, without hesitation, went up to the revolving restaurant, cancelled his reservation, went into the lounge and started drinking. After five doubles he decided it was time to leave and started on his way home. While walking to the LRT he was recognised by two drug dealers. Koreg was so drunk he didn't even know who they were.

"Hey, Kor lookin' good. Where'd you just come from the tower?" asked the bigger dude.

"Ya," he started to say something else but was interrupted with.

"Then you can obviously pay me back what you owe me," the dude lied.

Koreg was so drunk he couldn't remember if it was true or not, but he said, "look I just came from the bar and I've spent everything, it hasn't been a good night and I just want to go home. I'll see you later for that, you know."

"No, you'll see me now." And the guy punched him square in the forehead.

Knocking him unconscious, they rifled through his pockets and found his wallet. Looking through it, they found three hundred dollars and the ring. Kicking him a few times, they left him there. He didn't regain consciousness until the ambulance arrived and he found himself, again, in the hospital. He was released with a few broken ribs and a major headache.

March 26

Koreg's final hours were not pleasant by any means. His roommate blamed him for her arrest and wouldn't let him live it down. On this one particular day, she came to him and said she forgave him. She understood that he went through his own situation that night and wanted to forgive and forget. They both hugged and the plot was set in motion.

That night, there was a party. It was said to be a reunion and forgiveness party but, that was misleading and misdirection to make sure Koreg showed up. The plan was to get him as drunk as possible and take him to the park. There, they would leave him in the cold and have him find his own way back. It was meant to be a deadly practical joke because, he would either show up with frostbite or end up frozen to death. But things did not go as planned.

When they arrived at the park it was an unusually cold bitter night, minus twenty-two, they sat in the car for a few moments and smoked a joint. Then she suggested that Koreg and she go out for a walk, even though it was bitter cold, Koreg was so drunk he didn't even feel it. After leaving the car and walking for a while Koreg turned to try to give her a kiss but, to his dismay, he was struck with a bat on the back of the head. It stunned him, just for a moment, but when he recaptured himself the cold set in and sobered him up quickly.

He always carried his knife and he pulled it, swinging at the person who had hit him with the bat, missing. She was closer than she thought and he slashed her face cutting into her eye. She fell to the ground and started whimpering, "Oh my god."

The guy with the bat swung again and brought the bat down on the top of Koreg's head crushing his skull in and knocking him unconscious. The two ran back to the car. She was bleeding profusely and they sped to the hospital as fast as possible.

Koreg lay in the cold, bleeding and unconscious, never regaining consciousness. Koreg froze to death in the spot where his soul, ghost, now stands, in complete and utter depression, staring at the spot where his body was found, moaning in sadness.

Story 5
The Pond 2

I am only an observer at this time. While mulling around, watching one of my favourite characters, he vanished into the forest around one of the pond's streams. I began to hear voices, it was of children playing, this could only mean an encounter. When this character gets excited he disperses into a fog-like state until ready for the event.

What this does is strengthens the entity giving a reinforcement to manifest and be seen, at will, to his victims. In this case the parents of these two young children. Where there are children there is a potential happening and this one is to be remembered.

The day had started off warm and breezy, which meant, there would be a change early in the day. He liked that. It made for a more dramatic episode.

The children were playing a typical game of hiding and seek and what he liked to do is join in on their fun. There were only two so his intervention was necessary. It gave the game more intrigue and made the trap more suspenseful.

He stepped out from behind a bush and introduced himself. "Hey," he said to the girl. They are always the most curious and willing to make him a part of their fun.

"Hey," she replied.

"What are you playing?" he asked.

"Hide and seek," she looked puzzled not knowing where he had come from. "Where did you come?" she questioned.

"Over there," she pointed towards the pond and the little stream that trickled into it.

"Who are you looking for," he quizzed.

"My brother; he's hiding somewhere, and I have to find him," she exclaimed.

"I'll help."

And they both started wandering through the grouping of trees in search of her brother. Finding him, inside a hollowed-out log, she introduced them, and the character asked if he could join them. They agreed and made him the "it" person. He began counting, and the two ran off into the thickest part of the wooded area.

Dad and mom were at the picnic table preparing the food, as he was setting up the BBQ, she asked, "Have you seen the kids? I haven't heard them in quite a while, and I'm wondering if they are okay."

"They're playing in the woods, and if one of them is hurt, I'm sure we'd know about it by now. Let's just give them their time and get things ready."

"Okay."

So they carried on with the task of sorting and dividing. In the forest, the kids hid themselves very well, but he knows this forest, he has been here a long time. It's his home.

He started wandering off in the opposite direction, just to give them more time to bury themselves.

This is his game and most times the children are found in the same places he knows well. These kids though are a little cleverer he began to search but in vain. They had hidden themselves so well he had no idea where he was to look.

When he finally found them, they had dropped themselves in a hole. That put him at an advantage, and he began to toy with them. First, because they were so deep, threatening to bury them. But decided instead to throw dried leaves on top of them and set them on fire.

The boy, while dropping into the hole, had twisted his ankle pretty bad but, said nothing, wanting to play out this game. His sister, seeing what was happening, saw that there is an exit, the hole turned out to be a cramped cave, just to the left of the cave and crawled out to find her parents.

As the parents were about ready to find the kids, the little girl came running out of the trees screaming, "Daaaad, come quick Tommy's in trouble. He's fighting with a boy, and the boy is trying to set him on fire."

"Where are they?"

"In the woods, by a small pond and Tommy's stuck in a cave."

Both parents began running towards the pond following the daughter. When they reached the hole Tommy was gone. They started yelling his name to hear if he would answer and heard nothing.

Searching, it took almost an hour but finally found his lifeless body along the pond's edge. Just as the dad was reaching to pull him out, "Bam" in the back of the head, It was a branch, and he fell face first into the water.

Lifting himself up and looking along the shoreline, he saw a little boy, about fourteen years old, holding a large branch, "What the hell are you trying to prove?" Dad yelled.

The boy just ran laughing and reaching the mom, hit her in the face. She went down as blood spurted all around her. The dad saw that she was not moving and feared the worst. As he came upon her, he saw she was still breathing but knocked unconscious. He reached down to pick her up, but as he did "Bam" again, he fell and this time there was a gash on his head.

Bleeding he scrambled to his feet picked up his wife and headed to the car placing her in it, "I'm going to get Rachel and call 911, wait here."

He went back to the woods and started calling her. Nothing. Frantically, he started running through the woods, and as though a ghost, she crawled out of a hollow log. Grabbing her up, he began running back to the car, but then "Bam" again, he was hit from behind. He dropped his daughter to the ground and fell face first into the tree in front of him.

Opening his eyes, he sees the boy holding the branch, "Why are you doing this!" he yelled.

The boy laughed, and in an instant, the boy was right in front of him, like blinking speed, and he had hit him again, this time in the face across his eyes.

Blinded, he yelled at Rachel, "Go to the car with your mom."

Wiping the dirt from his eyes, yet still barely able to see, he staggered to his feet and began heading towards the car. It seemed like an hour but it was just a few minutes. When he got there both his wife and daughter were unconscious, It appeared as though someone had beaten them with a baseball bat or, the branch that the boy had, he could only assume.

As he turned to see where he was the car door slammed into him and he fell backwards, his hand getting caught in the closing of it.

Somehow, the car started and automatically went into gear. Bewildered, he franticly tried to open the car door as he was being dragged towards the boat launch.

It was a slow-moving speed but gradually increased as it neared the launch. The car nosed its way to the crest and the wheels turned as it entered onto the downslope. He couldn't even scream as he fought, in vain, to release his hand.

Then "splash" and the car went into the water. It didn't sink right away giving him ample time to open the door.

Standing in the water he turned to the shoreline seeing the boy standing there. Puzzled, chest deep, he started towards the shore, it was a tough walk as the rocks were slimy and the water cold. Then "Bam," a rock struck him on the forehead.

Blood began pouring into his eyes and he was partially blinded again, then another hit him on the temple and he went down. He was close enough to the shore that the boy could start hitting him in the head as he drifted along the shore. After a few battering's, the dad didn't appear to be moving so the boy stopped.

The boy just stood there observing and ruminating over the bodies. He began to contemplate how much of a fight the dad had been and how the others were so submissive. It was as though they gave themselves to him without question, accepting their fate with no malice. It was intense and he felt at peace.

Just then the police rolled into the parking lot and circled around to the launch.

"We have a situation down here," came a voice from the car. "It's a 10-100 and there's a car in the pond."

"We're going to need a coroner down here and a tow truck."

"Copy that, what's your 20."

"Schynstyk pond parking lot. It's not a nice scene, it looks like this guy drowned himself and floated out of the open door. I don't see anything else but the car is completely submerged."

"We'll have a backup there in fifteen minutes."

"Ten-four."

The tow truck arrived before the backup so he and the policeman, at the scene, began to observe the car and the best way to get it out of the pond. As the other police arrived the tow truck driver was suiting up to go in to hook up the wince when he noticed other bodies floating in the back seat, "Hey, there are others in here."

Hooking up the car he signalled to the cop to start the wince. It whined with a high pitch squeal and then the car jerked into motion with a crunch and scraping across the bumper. Dan got out of the water as the car was slowly pulled from the pond.

After getting it off the ramp and into the parking lot he opened the front door and as the water drained from inside the bodies of the mother and daughter was discovered. When Dan and the cop looked in they could see the trauma of the blunt force that killed them.

The coroner had been there just before the car was pulled from the pond, and he waited till the investigation team gave the okay to tag them and bag them.

The sergeant didn't want to leave the park until there was a thorough scout around the park for possible others. It took twenty minutes but they found the son at the edge of the pond in the forested area. It looked as though he suffered from a broken neck and some blunt force lacerations.

It was concluded after the autopsy that the father must have gone on a rampage and killed his whole family. They concluded that his trauma was caused by the mom as she, in self-defence, tried to protect herself.

Story 6
Lake Schynstyk

There are some of us that are caught in certain areas, because they are twisted. These are poltergeists that are brutal, they are the most dominant. Their energy is about brute force, but it can take a wrong turn and be used against them, draining the entity of all his energy, if their energy is directed without fulfilment. Instead, the ghoul becomes the target.

It's about how many victims and how fast they can overpower them. The longer they wait for a target the angrier they become. Joey is one of those phantoms. He chooses to stay in his field, the only one he patrols. Finding trouble, not just with the solids he stocks, but with other mischievous spirits. That's what he likes. We refer to the living as solids. Yet, what solids don't know is, we can be hurt. Joey found this out during a day of stalking a target. He didn't act in a timely manner and he got caught in his own quagmire of energy.

After stalking his victim he was in the process of attack when this person came into his domain, from behind, and proceeded to flail his arms, violently, into the air. Joe just happened to be in the right place, with his back turned, and "BAM". He got the first blow to his head. Feeling lightheaded and before he could recover "crack", aboard broke on his back and he was down. It isn't the board that takes him down but, the lack of acting before the contest begins.

There is one thing I have to tell you, once a contest has started, that's what we like to call them, there is no stopping it. Even though the assaulter, he or she, doesn't know they are beating an entity figure. This guy is relentless, he starts stomping the ground and Joe is right there taking it. Joey knows he had the power to avoid it, but, it's all about timing, isn't it.

Finding his way to a grouping of trees, he goes to where there were killings and dead bodies under its grounds. This is a bad idea, people, like this guy, are drawn to where there was a violent act and, it just so happens that he, the abuser, decided to run a drop kick at the tree and you know who's standing there? Joey. The first drop kick sent him into the tree he was standing in front of but, it was the second one that put Joey into a senseless motion of torment.

The assailant started stomping on the ground, again where Joey was laying. You see, even when we're broken it's only a state of mind, we can still move. It can be excruciatingly painful but, only if we want to feel it. Untimely for Joe, it's the difference of being right where he needed to be or not.

He must be feeling it, like being in hell's fury and not being able to find your way out. The thing is, we can't die. Joe has to take it until this person is finished, which is usually the case for everyone, and this guy was hyped and would not stop. No one has ever gone through this for so long and it was so punishing we didn't even notice when the knife was pulled. We did see the first cut, it was one of the deepest, and he wasn't finished. Without hesitation he started stabbing the ground, and yes there was Joe.

Joe was cut into pieces, but only because he let it happen, when the contest finishes, Joe wouldn't look like he had gone through this episode. He didn't, really feel the pain it is a memory from his past life. By being in the wrong place with the wrong mind set, Joey was brought into a whirlwind of tormented frustration and anxious anxiety. What we found out later he was a mercenary and he was going through his routine before departing for another mission.

Story 7
The Brook

They walked the path together, holding hands, until they came to a crossing. The crossing was a fallen tree that jutted out across the brook, only one-third of the brook was crossed by the tree; the end of the crossing was several smaller logs that, in comparison, looked like branches. They decided to challenge it any way, being that the parking lot was on the other side, just over the hill.

The width of the tree was thick enough but they had to cross one behind the other or they would be off balance and surely fall in. It looked safe enough, as they decided to try it. The branches were still somewhat fresh and the new growth made it look easy. What could happen?

"Let's take this instead of walking the whole way around," he said smiling at her. She looked at him apprehensively and nodded okay. Stepping onto the large log he almost lost his balance and grabbed a branch that was an offshoot of new growth. "Wow that was a close one," he whispered under his breath. He has a terrible fear of water and the last thing he needed was to fall into the swift-running brook, not knowing the depth of it or the strength of the current.

After gaining his footing he reached out to her and encouraged her to join him and she did. Though there were only smaller logs completing the gap on the other side they felt confident as they stumbled their way across the large log. Stopping, they both stared at each other.

"Did you hear that?" she said with surprise.

"Ya," he retorted. They both turned, looking behind them, on the side of the log they had climbed onto stood two children staring back at them.

"You're going to drown if you fall in," the older one said grinning.

"Ya," the little girl answered in agreement.

"Well, that's not going to happen," he exclaimed and they both continued making their way across the log.

Their eyes had been set on the log's path, the branches they held onto to kept their balance, and they were startled to notice there were two other kids on the far side, where the gap was completed by smaller and looser logs. "Where did these kids come from," he said under his breath looking up at his girlfriend.

"Ya, it's as though they just appeared out of nowhere," she replied in the same manner. He was in a stoop reaching to grab another branch and stood up smiling and waved at the two other boys who were standing at the shoreline.

"Hey, how you doin'?" he said loudly, to overcome the roar of the water as it roared past the log. The shoreline, where the boys were, was at a distance and that was also an issue that he had to consider as well. The boys smiled and waved back as they continued their trek making their way towards them. The kids on the other side were taller and both had a smirk, they both questioned, with a glance at each other.

"We'll be okay, we don't need help" he exclaimed waving them to stay where they were. As he was doing so the tallest boy started climbing onto the smaller logs and began making his way towards them.

"What the hell is he doing he whispered to her?" she shrugged and they continued to move forward awkwardly reaching for each branch and new growth to maintain balance. They both could faintly hear the other two, on the side they climbed onto, giggling and whispering to each other.

As they were nearing the middle of the large log one of the boys, now on the large log, motioning them to stay where they are. The boy who climbed the other side said, "I'll be there to help in a second."

"We're okay, just go back, there isn't room for the three of us and it will be more hazardous. Just go back," he said abruptly, and all he heard was, "I'm almost there," came the reply from the tallboy.

As they reached the midpoint of the stream the log started to narrow and keeping balance was becoming more difficult, there was moss growing on it as well, something they didn't count on, and it became hard to find grip. She slipped a couple of times and he had to help her regain balance, almost pulling the both of them in. Both being non-swimmers, that would have been a treacherous and deadly incident; still, they managed to make it to the middle of the log where the boy met them both.

"Hey" he greeted them, with a questionable look, "We need to get past you how is this going to be done," the boy immediately grabbed both by the jackets and fell backwards into the brook. The shock of the cold water and the surprise of the boy's action caused them to let out all the air from their lungs and they both splashed into the stream breathless. The brook, at this time of the year, was more like a river, due to hard rains and melting snow. The torrent of the current made it impossible to fight the boy and gain control and all three were dragged downstream into the pond. The boy was strong and had pulled them deep into the brook making it difficult for either of them to catch their breath. By the time they reached the pond they were both unconscious and the boy pulled them into the depth of the pond where they both lay lifeless at the bottom.

The three remaining kids had mounted the crossing and made their way to the middle of the brook to watch the event. After the excitement was over, they looked at each other and said, "That was lame, they hardly struggled that was too quick why didn't they fight harder?" the little girl enquired.

"I don't know," the smaller of the two boys on the log said.

"Maybe they wanted to die," the second boy intervened.

"No, I think they didn't know how to swim and after they fell in they were done."

"Oh," the little girl replied.

On the far side of the smaller logs, the larger boy stood and whistling he yelled, "Come on; it's over what are you waiting for Christmas?" They all laughed, got to their feet and started across to the smaller and looser tree ends, reaching the shoreline, as they stepped off the crossing and their feet hit the ground, they each disappeared.

Later that week as a little boy and his sister were playing around the pond, they noticed something floating along the shoreline. They both ran down to see what it might be, reaching the shoreline they discovered it was the body of a girl. Running back to where her dad was BBQing, "Dad…Dad," the little girl screamed excitedly, "come quick there's someone in the water and she's not moving."

Her brother was in the foreground waving his arms and pointing towards the shoreline yelling "Dad…dad! It's a girl," the dad then picked up his cell and dialled 911, as he walked to the edge of the water to see what they were so excited about.

When the police arrived, they determined that she had been in the water for about a week. They began searching to discover in a nearby brush, one hundred yards down from where the girl was discovered, a man was also found.

As they searched and found their identification, they realised that the man was the owner of the car at impound towed several days before.

Speculating, they came to the conclusion, that this was a horrible accident happening as they were crossing the stream on the tree. "They must have slipped and fallen in drowning. The cold water would have put their bodies into shock, hypothermia would then set in, they wouldn't have had a chance one of the officers exclaimed. "That isn't a brook anymore it's the size of a river and people are determined to challenge that tree crossing just to shave off a few minutes of walking time."

"Ya," another interjected. "This is the third time this season; I think we should put in a request to have that crossing removed." Cleaning the area and removing the bodies they were taken to autopsy. when the coroner finished the autopsy he declared it as a misfortunate accident. The consideration of removing the crossing fell on deaf ears and it remains in place.

"People just have to be more careful when taking this route but the brook for most of the year is not dangerous and is quite safe to be around," said one of the officers in observation.

Story 8
The Running Shoe

He started putting on his first shoe, grinning, he thought to himself, "The first of a long line of style," He had just been approved, by Nike, with his design for the exclusive summer edition. His design would be the focus of this year's iconic style. This is a special day for him. The pair he has is first off the production line and the first to be worn by anyone. As he prepared himself for his daily evening jog he again admired himself in them, in the mirror on the wall, just as you enter the front door.

Leaving, he toyed with the feel of the soul, under his foot, before setting off on his route. The route was a five-mile jog that took him past a small stream of water in Schynstyk Park. He did this jog every day, but today was a special day. Today he had his iconic Nike's on and they were the greatest feeling he could ever have had.

She was a little girl at the time of her accident. She and her brother were playing beside the stream. Just a simple game of rock jumping that went awry. It started out at the top of the stream, where it's a small outcropping from the brook, which flows to the lake. They were jumping innocently across the stream from one large rock to another.

Her brother then came up with an idea, "Why don't we make a game of this. Jump from one large rock to the other, one side of the stream to the other and see how far we get before we run out of rocks or the stream becomes too wide."

She agreed, it sounded fun and adventurous, enough to want to challenge it. It started off easy, one rock was at most, one step from the other and the shoreline was always close, but as they got further downstream it began to widen. The rocks had become fewer and became a greater distance apart. As the stream widened there were more tributaries making the stream deeper as well. They were so caught in the fun of the game that, before they both were aware of the vastness of the stream, it was too late. She was stuck and the rock she was on was unstable, her fear paralysed her.

Her brother, in his excitement, took off to find their dad. It took him twenty minutes to find him and, after a roller-coaster explanation, they both ran back to the shoreline to find her but, when they arrived, she was not there. Nor was the rock she was perched on.

"Are you playing games with me?" his father asked in frustration.

"No, she was right there on a rock."

"First off where's the rock and second, where's your sister."

His father asked with confusion. Starting to cry, he said, "She was right there." The dad started calling for her with no response so they started searching the area she would most likely be in from that point of the brook. Nothing, not a sound, standing there all they could hear was the brushing of the grass and trees against the wind, a few birds overhead and the babbling of the brook.

They called in the police and did a major search, yet again, found nothing. The next day the search team dragged the brook and still came up empty. All that was found is one running shoe along the shoreline several metres down from where she had been, perched on the shoreline.

So the police started asking questions, confronting the boy and the dad as though they might be hiding the truth. After a week of interrogation, everything was dismissed and she was listed as a runaway. There was no funeral, no media coverage just her picture on a milk bottle and the silence of not having her in their lives.

What had happened is, she again tried to reach a smaller rock with her foot and the one she was on moved. Because of the weight imbalance, she fell into the water and sank. The rock she was on also did a roll, with the current of the brook and buried her underneath it.

The only way they would have found the body would be to lift the rock, from its new resting place, to pull her from beneath it. How could anyone have known?

With her death, she vowed revenge, "*How could they have left me there? Why did no one come to rescue me? It's as though I was forgotten, unwanted and left to die. They will play and die.*" And she waited.

As he entered the park he felt a gentle breeze brush across his face, against the warmth of the sun, it made the run more enjoyable. He also thought he heard the giggle of a little girl, but dismissed it believing it to be in his head. Yet, it seemed so real and seemed to come from further down the path, "Na," he thought to himself.

The day was so hot, the gentle breeze coming off the lake made the heat less consuming. The breeze helped him to embrace the moment and enjoy the beauty of the park on the path he was jogging on.

As he approached the area, where the little girl met her unfortunate demise, it came again, "Tee, hee, hee," except this time it was right beside him. He stopped dead in his tracks, "Who's there," he questioned, getting nothing in return. He looked around quizzically and seeing nothing he continued on the path except he was walking, not running, hoping to maybe see who it was that might be following him.

As he looked over his shoulder, for the thirteenth time, something tripped him. It felt like a little foot, he couldn't be sure cause when looking around, there was nothing. Brushing it off, "It must have been my own feet," he chuckled to himself aloud.

He continued walking and just as he took his first stride, to continue his run, he was again tripped. "What the…" he fell to the ground scraping his knees and thigh and crunching his face on the gravel covered path.

"Fuuuuck," his hands were also scraped and chalked with tinny pebbles.

"Who's doing this," he yelled to the breeze.

And the giggle came again, right beside him, in his ear. As he quickly pivoted on his left leg, he felt a heavy push and tripped off the path onto the shoreline and onto some large rocks that were sitting behind the stone curb. It was a small drop of about three feet, but far enough to do some damage.

As he hit the rocks his right arm flung out, instinctively to save himself from the fall but hit the rock in an unnatural twist. Hearing a crack and crunch of bone, as he again smashed his face, scraping his left arm on another large rock, he skewed to the left, just before the shoreline. Rolling into the brook he inhaled a mouth full of water.

But for the gagging, choking and coughing, he wanted to let out a hateful questioning scream. Confused and heavily shaken he knew his wrist and arm were broken; his face fractured and possibly suffering from a minor concussion. Soaked and standing in the water, with the current racing around his waist, he began to move towards the shoreline. The water was cold enough that it prevented him from feeling the pain in his leg and by dangling his hand. It was also eased from pain.

The rocks were sharp and full of brown algae which made the trek back to the shore precarious. As he reached the shoreline, something, or someone, grabbed his hair and he fell backwards into the brook again, this time hitting his head on a large bolder. The rock could not be seen, as it was several inches under the water. It didn't even show the cause of a current wave.

With the help of her pulling his hair he hit the rock hard again, swallowing a mouthful of water that went directly into his lungs and stomach and he started choking. Gagging, trying to get back on his feet, his broken right wrist and arm were so painful that to grab at the rock was impossible so, all he could do is try to reach out to the bottom of the brook, with his left arm.

Although the brook was only waist deep, finding his footing was frustrated by the brown algae that had grown around the rocks. Reaching down, the only hold he could find was the bedrock and the bolder he had bashed his head on.

Grabbing franticly at the bottom of the bolder he wedged his hand underneath it and the rock moved, just a fraction, crushing his hand under it and wedging it there so he had no way to find release. Wincing with the pain, he took his final breath filling his lungs with water. In the turbulence of the brook and his excitement, he lost one of his running shoes.

That afternoon, as an older couple walked the path, the running shoe was found washed up on the shoreline. The only reason they took notice of it was because of its newness and different look of techno sheen. After going missing, for a week, a search party found his body, still submerged, with his hand crushed under the rock. His hand had to be detached before they could remove him from the brook.

At the autopsy, the doctors determined that his death was accidental but, were shocked by the condition of the corpse. With the broken bones, scrapes and head injuries, it appeared as though he were in a fight with several combatants. But, when the police did their investigation there was no evidence of it. Closing the case it was determined that he must have fallen hard, rolled into the brook and caught his hand under the rock. It was a frightening, mysterious and tragic accident.

Story 9
The Second Pond
The Fishing Rod

He was walking along the path that crested the shoreline. Stopping at an observation point he, after reading the information plaque, stood to look over the pond and recognised some of the wildlife he read about on the plaque.

As he scanned the shoreline he noticed, just ten yards away from where he stood, a stick-like object cresting just below the waterline. It was in a position that, if one did not look long enough, it would easily be overlooked or, because it was in a place that was just out of reach. No one would take the time to pull it from its place of discovery. He, on the other hand, is always curious of things. If he sees something out of place he has to discover why or how it came to be where it is.

Wading out to the object he began to realise the pond is deeper than first observed and when he was at the reaching point, he found himself chest deep.

When reaching out to pull the end of the object out, which he observed to be the end of a machined pole or stick, he slipped, but it felt more like a push. He didn't know how to swim and the water is deep. As well, the cloths he had on were heavy with water and he went under like a sack of rocks, and that was it. He never tried to push himself from the bottom, he couldn't, his clothes were too heavy. He never tried to grab anything to prevent himself from sinking, he just went down. It's like he wanted to die. Most people at least, try to fight to live, but him, he just drowned.

Story 10
Ghosted

She has returned after being away at university. Ravishing and enchanting a haunting reminder of youth. The energy that she gives and takes, her smile, her laugh, vibrant and alive a possession that few have.

She is an entrancing Asian beauty who had grown up in an urban district. Her parents were of high esteem and affluent in the Asian community. She was adventurous, and after a few years at a university, she decided to take some time off. She thought she might like to travel or, maybe get into business just to find her passion of interest. While, in her travels, she found a quaint little town and decided to stay.

She had gotten involved with a man who was running a community shelter for the homeless and the elderly. She applied herself as a volunteer while also working in a children s group home. While volunteering, at the shelter, she met the owner and they began a friendship, in a short time it became more and they moved into a flat together. Months became years and years became ten and more numbering sixteen. Throughout that time, they were married and had a child.

The past three years were difficult as grants started to diminish because, businesses took on other interests and, government funding became less due to the recession. Together they decided to sell the shelter and make changes. That's when she came up with the suggestion to move back to her parents' place, to find a new beginning, in the city where she grew up. He agreed and over the next few months they made arrangements to move.

It was difficult at first, finding themselves in a tight dwelling shared with her elderly parents while searching for their own place, was not in vain. They found a townhouse a short distance from her parents and began the adjustment of their new life.

They talked about having their own dinner, it would be a quaint little restaurant located in a plaza where it would serve the business area and the community with delivery. It took several years before finding the right location and surprisingly it was close to home, several miles south of their residence. As they began to settle into the routine of their new life, she thought she would reintroduce herself to old acquaintances and learn about where their lives had taken them.

Change had taken her into a different look she had changed her hair colour to blond and it suited, complimented, her in looks and in age making her appear more youthful and well maintained. In her search for friends, she came to a place where she discovered an old boyfriend who had once shared a moment of lust and flirted with love. The place was a martial arts studio where he taught.

So she decided to inquire about enrolling her son and reacquaint herself with him, out of interest in his life and just to feed her curiosity.

Entering the studio she observed him working with a student on the mat and gave a little wave, "hi," she said with a little grin. "How are you?"

"Hi," he exchanged and asked her to join him for a brunch at the cafe on the corner. She agreed and they went to talk so they could catch up on what they had been doing since they last were together.

She told him about where she had moved to and how her life had taken a different path than expected. Not finishing University had put a strain on her relationship with her parents and through the years they became more and more distant Then, after talking it over with her husband, they decided to move back to start fresh and rebuild the relationship between her and her parents.

Looking at her watch she found that she had taken up too much time and needed to return to the restaurant. They made plans to see each other the next day and maybe spend some time together on the weekend, just to get comfortable and maybe she could give pointers on how to expand his business into something larger. She agreed and felt good about the connection she had just made and felt she could give some insight into expansion and make it a bigger enterprise.

He, after they had gone their separate ways, began to mull over their coming together and thought, "How fair she had maintained herself," and he wanted her. The deception has to be clear. He started to contemplate the plan and realised, he has the perfect consideration for his business, to bring her in as a consultant would be the perfect ploy for his intentions.

That weekend, when they met, he invited her back to his studio, to go over plans for the expansion he had been working on. Hesitant, because of costs and personal circumstances, entering the studio he motioned to the desk, where his plans were located, and looking quite disorderly. She walked over and started to go through the mess, asking, "What have you decided to do about finding another studio and, where would you like it to be?"

She hadn't noticed that he had closed the curtains on the large window and dimmed the lights locking the door as well. He walked over to her, as she included "I have had some training in tie chi and would like to, maybe, go into more training, after I enrol my son with you, as well."

Standing behind her, he said, "why don't we go over some of the routines and I can get an idea of what you know and where to begin."

"Okay," and she walked to the centre of the mat and stood waiting for instruction. He then began taking her through some exercises and started to get closer and more personable, helping her through the moves and telling her, "Your clothing is too restrictive," and began removing her shirt. He then continued by removing her pants until she was in her bra and panties.

She was lying on the mat, with him over top of her. He began removing his clothes as well, pinning her to the ground with his weight. She was so stunned she didn't know how to react, the studio was large and if she screamed, she knew no one would hear. So she just let it happen.

After he had taken advantage of her, she couldn't look at him and she wanted to get out of there as quickly as possible, but he wouldn't let her leave. Instead, he made her sit and have a tea, "I have longed for you since we first dated but, you disappeared. When I asked your parents where you had gone, they just smiled and said she'd be in touch soon.

"But for now, she has just gone and didn't give a place to send mail or communicate from. It was like they thought I was the reason you'd left. Like you were running from me? Is this true?" He looked at her body movements to see if she would reveal anything that would give an acknowledging sign. But she just sat there in silence and stared.

He continued, "I want this to continue. You are to tell no one and, we will meet here once a week, even if just to talk or go over plans for diversification. I have loved you, in secret, though I did not know where you were. I have waited and I knew, if you were to return, it is because we were meant to be together. Soul mates if you will."

She shrugged and even though she knew she had just been raped. There was a sense of exhilaration, and, a thrill that he had such feelings for her all this time.

As she was leaving, she didn't turn to look at him, instead, she began to contemplate her arrival at the cafe. Would they know, could anyone tell, did she appear different? Entering the cafe everything was normal. No one gave any indication of knowledge and she just went on about business in her normal manner.

Over the next few months, she met him regularly as he had demanded and he told her that if she ever missed, he would come down to the cafe and destroy everything and take her. Everyone would know then that she is his and there is nothing they could do about it.

This meeting went on for nine months. On this one Saturday, though, the studio was empty. He had moved, just disappeared. He had said nothing to her and with a sigh of relief, she felt that it was finally over.

The affair had taken its toll on her marriage. She was distant with her husband, uninvolved with her son, and easily agitated. There was very little or no intimacy between her and her husband and when approached she would blow off as though he was getting ready to rape her.

They went through the new year without incident but just before valentine's day she got a call on her cell, It was him, "Hello," she answered.

"Hey, I'm back in town. I've moved the studio to a place about several hours outside of the city. It took a few months to get settled but I am back and ready to continue with our engagement."

She started to shake uncontrollably and almost fainted. She had thought that he would not return, his interaction with her was impulsive and erratic.

"I want you to meet with me, today; there is a coffee shop just outside the studio. It will take you two hours to get there, I timed it. If I have to come and get you, I will destroy everything you own and everyone will know what is going on between us. It's 1 o'clock now so I'll be expecting you here no later than 3:30," hanging up she began to think.

"What have I got myself into," she grabbed a sweater and her purse and left. Getting into the car her husband pulled in behind her.

"Where are you off to?" he inquired.

"I've got some business to take care of with an old friend and I won't be back for a few hours. Make dinner, and I'll see you then." Her husband went in and started to contemplate on who it could be but couldn't bring anyone to mind.

As she was driving, she wondered what this was all about and what it was going to lead to, if the affair is to continue. Pulling into the town she found the coffee shop within a few minutes and parked. Checking the time she noticed that she was early and sat there, contemplating just what she might be in for. He is a manipulative and violent individual and would not be able to avoid anything he might try to impress her with.

Entering the coffee shop she saw him seated in the back facing the door, he could see everyone coming and going. He held his arm up just to let her know she had been seen and motioned her to join him.

Sitting down he said, "I've taken the consideration to order for you, it will be here in a few minutes and, you will sit there and listen to what I have to say." She began shaking as he continued, "You are mine, I have been waiting for your return for years and here you are. We are soul mates, just as the saying goes, in love, you must let it go, if it returns it is true, if she does not it was never meant to be. You have returned.

"We are meant to be together. I have loved you for a very long time and could have looked for you but, I left it alone to see if you would return on your own, and, you have. Now I am letting you know how it is going to be for us," he quieted himself as the order was placed in front of them and began again, when he was satisfied, they were unobserved, "This is how it is going to go down.

"Whenever I call, you are to meet me at the place I have arranged. If you are late there will be consequences. Consequences I will not disclose until I feel it necessary," she had finished her tea and appetisers and he began again:

"Let us go for a walk. There is a park just half mile from here, you will leave your car and we'll take mine," getting up she couldn't help but feel the emotion overwhelm her and she began to tear. Daintily taking a napkin she wiped them away without being noticed by him walking with him to his car.

Arriving at the park, they both got out together and strolled over to the walking path. He reached out to hold her hand but she resisted and he turned to her and said, "consequences, if you do not let me do the things, I desire your husband will meet me, and it won't be pleasant. The first time will just be a meeting of the minds; it will get worse after that. Things will get broken, bones, items of personal value."

She held his hand, and they began to walk. He began pointing out the beauty of the place he had chosen and why he settled here. She tried her best to hold back the tears while he explained how their lives were intertwined with all of this beauty.

They came to a meadow and he turned to her and kissed her. She was surprised at the way her body reacted, a rush of excitement, something she didn't expect to feel. His hands went under her sweater and he began disrobing her, whispering in her ear he said, "Do not resist. No one comes here at this time, so, we are alone. I want to make love to you now and, you will not resist."

He continued to take off her clothes until she and he were completely naked. He brought her to her knees and motioned her head to his hardness. She took him into her mouth and began the motions of his expectations. He ejaculated in her mouth and he told her to swallow it. He then lay her down on the grass and, surprising to her, he was still erect and he entered her.

While they were engaging, she thought she heard some voices off in the distance and thought to scream but, realised it would be a mistake and just stayed silent. He had rolled her over, to face the ground, and put her in the position of all fours and entered, between her legs, from behind. He then asked her if she was clean and she said yes. He removed his hardness from her and bent down over her nakedness and, with his tongue, began licking her between her cheeks and legs.

When he was sure she was moist enough he entered her button. When he did, a rush went through her like she had never felt before, and, she orgasmed, while he began the stimulus of himself again. She began to moan with the pleasure of this, not knowing why; she began to give herself to him with the motions of excitement and the feelings of orgasmic stimulation and emotionalism.

She rolled onto her back and, keeping him inside her, began to move with him in a passion she had never felt before. She felt the moment of his release and she, in turn, orgasmed again. He then entered her between her legs, and in a few moments became hard again.

They both moved in unison, while she succumbed to his desire, with every breath-taking moment. He entered her button again, moving between each desired access, they both again reached a climax together. He fell on top of her for a moment, to catch himself, and she relaxed perplexed by her own astonishment of the circumstance.

They both looked at each other and he, smiling said, "This is the way I always felt it would be."

Sheepishly, she grinned and began putting on her clothes. He drove her back to her car and, without and word exchanged, she got in and watched while he went back to his studio.

On her way home, she began to contemplate what had occurred and couldn't stop the tears from happening. She realised he had again, continued with his rape of her, but wondered why she felt the passion while in the moment. All she wanted was the silence of the car's wheels bringing her home so she could shower the disgust, of him, off her. Looking at the car clock and noticing the time, she realised, she had been with him for five hours and it was getting dark. She would not be home before 10:00 or 10:30.

When she finally arrived, all she wanted to do is a shower and go to bed. Dinner had been finished hours before, but she couldn't eat anything and wanted to try to forget the whole circumstance but she knew it would only continue. She showered and went to bed without exchanging any conversation with her husband. Although he felt something wrong thought better of perusing any inquiry and joined her in bed.

The next few weeks went by without incident. She didn't hear from him and nothing was questioned by her husband. As she started to relax and got back into the routine of the coffee shop things started to feel normal again, until she answered the phone, while at the front of the cafe. It was him.

"I want you," came the voice on the other side. "I left you alone so as not to arouse suspicion or question. But I have to see you, now. I have made reservations at a nearby motel it is easy to find and the room I chose is discrete. You can enter from the street at the back of the building unobserved."

She looked around the cafe to see if anyone was suspicious of the call as he went on, "The room is 102, and there is a small corridor blocking vision from all other rooms and the front office. It should only take you one and a half-hour to get there, it's for the night so I'll be waiting. I want you there no later than ten. Remember there are consequences for lateness as well as no show." He hung up.

She lingered on the line for a few moments, in contemplation. Strangely, she felt excited and fear as well.

She excused herself from the cafe and told her husband that she needed some time alone to go over some paperwork and meet with a friend for a few hours. Unsuspecting, he agreed and she left. Getting into the car, she began to wonder what he was planning and knew, after the last encounter it was anything but conversation.

Looking at her clock, she observed 5:10 and wondered if this was going to be like the last time. She found the motel easily, as he had said. She went to the room, knocked, and the voice on the other side said, "come in," it was him. He motioned her to join him at the table and she did. He poured her a tea.

"Have you relaxed and enjoyed your freedom of time away from me?"

She nodded, and he slapped her. "That's not the answer I want. You will say no and answer with you missed me."

"I have missed you and wondered why you hadn't called. I was going to make the call to see you but thought better of it. You must have your reasons and dismissed the idea to wait for you to get a hold of Me," she lied.

"Good, we have time so let's go for a walk and talk about what you have been doing over these past few weeks. They went outside to a nearby playground and she sat on a swing as he asked, "Have you been fucking your husband?" She nodded yes and he slapped her.

"Good, you must keep up relations with him so as not to arouse suspicion," he told her and put his hands on her breast.

"I love touching you; your skin is so smooth. You have kept yourself in good form over the years. I've been meaning to say that to you. Your husband must be keeping you well-financed to be able to maintain yourself like this."

She nodded not knowing what to expect from him as she did. "Is the shop gaining popularity?"

Again she nodded not knowing if that was the right answer.

But he just went on with, "Good, the business must stay well so you don't have problems leaving or sustaining yourselves and us. My studio has suffered a bit but I can offer you money if you need it."

She nodded yes and said, "I will need gas to get home."

He put four hundred dollars in her hand, taking it, even though it made her feel dirty. She felt compensation from the last encounter and for what was planned for this time.

They had left the park and were standing outside the room, as he closed the door he said, "Have a seat at the table and I'll make tea."

Serving her he stood behind her, putting his hands down her sweater, he began massaging her breasts. He then pulled the sweater over top of her head and undid her bra. She took a few sips of the tea but was overwhelmed with his caressing and massaging. As he turned the chair to face his torso, she knew what he wanted.

Undoing his belt and letting his pants drop to the floor, she put her hands into his underwear and pulled out his hardness. She massaged his appendage with her hand for a few moments and then kissed it, spreading her lips; she licked him with her tongue and put him into her mouth. She held onto his testicles and caressed his button with her fingers. She then began stimulating his erection, taking him in full, almost making her choke each time.

After what seemed like an hour he orgasmed in her mouth, he instructed her not to swallow yet. Pulling her up to face him, he kissed her with the protein still in her mouth. This went on for a while and they both ended with it shared between them. She swallowed what was left, and he kissed her again, putting what was still in his mouth back into hers, she swallowed that as well.

He then removed her pants and, she, his shirt. Holding her by the waist they fell back on the bed together and he entered her, while she lay on her back.

He then turned her around, she, to be on top, and she began moving in the form of leg thrusts to keep the movement going. He then slipped himself from between her legs and, using his fingers and hardness, he toyed with her between her cheeks. She then helped him enter her button. She continued the movement, of thrusts, as he was inside her. She then fell onto the bed to be on all fours, this was done with him still inside her.

He pulled out of her as he moved around her, to be behind her, and entered her button again. He then said, "Wait," pulling out of her and leaving the bed, he went into the bathroom and came back with a toy. As he got back onto the bed, he started massaging her, between her legs, with the toy that vibrated. He entered it inside her and started licking her between her cheeks, entering her button with his tongue. Bringing himself to his knees he entered her button with his hardness, still toying between her legs, inside her with the vibrator.

He then gently pulled her around to be on her back, not stopping with the toy, not slipping out of her button, he continued with her. This time using the toy set on his shaft, rocking it with his hardness inside her button, the toy between her legs, inside her, moving in sync. His orgasm, again, made her orgasm as well. This was the most pleasure she had ever received, from intimate activity, in her life.

Even though she detested this person, there was something about this experience she really desired, looking forward to these moments. As they continued for the next year, he got more inventive and she even participated, bringing different toys to experiment with.

One Saturday, it seemed different. He was hesitant, as though he were waiting for something. It turned out to be someone. She was in the moment, with his erection inside her mouth, and there was a knock. He stopped her and went to the door.

"I would like you to meet Zyling. She is here upon request. I had been talking to her about you and she asked to meet you, bringing up the idea to join us." she felt the pinch of jealousy seething through her. She knew he had been intimate with Zyling, when he wasn't with her, and this stirred her insides like a mixing beater.

The woman walked over to her and, using her fingers, started playing with her hair and said, "She is everything you said, beautiful, with her blond hair. It works with her. Not sluttish like on most Asians," Zyling exclaimed as she bent over and kissed her lips.

She felt like getting up and leaving. He knew this, seeing the strain on her face, and reminded her of consequences. So she remained seated. Zyling then started to massage her breasts, while he pulled Zyling's shirt off. Zyling then knelt down to kiss and suck on her breasts as well.

Being turned, to be backwards on the chair, he walked over and put his hardness to her lips. She knew what he wanted and, taking him into her mouth, began to stimulate his hardness. Zyling continued massaging her breasts, Licking and kissing her down her back. Zyling then brought her to her knees, while still on the chair, and began licking between her cheeks and inside her button.

She began to moan, with a pleasure she had never known before. Zyling, with her fingers, began massaging her between her legs and inside her, with the motions of an erectile organ. She began to orgasm uncontrollably and moan with every motion of his hardness inside her mouth. After his orgasm Zyling turned and kissed her, sharing the protein in her mouth, feeling like ice cream between them, and tasting like mint as Zyling had put candy in her mouth moments before.

While kissing her, Zyling moved her to the bed and she fell back onto it.

While she had him in her mouth, Zyling had been undressing; at the same time, Zyling was kissing and licking her inside her button. After falling onto the bed she felt Zyling's nakedness and enjoyed the warmth of Zyling's breath on her neck. He had removed himself and sat on a chair, at the table, to watch.

Zyling was engaged at the moment, kissing her down her abdomen, torso and then between her legs, fingering her between her cheeks and entering her button.

Licking her between her legs, Zyling entered her with her tongue; she arched her back to take in the whole of Zyling's tongue and fingers. He tossed the toy onto the bed and Zyling grabbed it.

Turning it on, Zyling entered it into her button. While still licking her between her legs and entering her with her fingers, she couldn't help but orgasm multiple times. Zyling then turned to position herself in the 69 so Zyling's legs were where she could be made to do the same for her. She started licking and toying with Zyling, clumsy at first, but more audacious as she got comfortable.

This went on for quite some time before he entered the twosome. And then it got disturbing. He dismissed her, paying attention only to Zyling, he motioned her to sit and watch. She was there for only a moment, until she quickly got up, dressed and removed herself from the situation.

Going home she thought of the evening and couldn't believe she was jealous. Still, on the drive, she also noticed the time, 4 am. What was she going to say? But her husband never questioned and she knew he knew something was amiss. She also knew this was the beginning of the end of this affair. It had been going on for two years six months and the only thing going on was lost time and failing relations between her and her husband. She had been avoiding his needs, looking forward to the encounters with him.

She knew that every time they were together it could be classified as rape but, because she was also a willing participant, it would be difficult. It had to end. The threats, the manipulation of her time and the lack of interest in her family were beginning to show. How? She continued to meet them for the next six months. Sometimes it was both; other times, just him and a few times just Zyling.

This has to stop. Little did she know she would get the opportunity to expose the affair in the New Year. He had called her and started threatening to confront her husband, to expose the affair, and she put him on speaker so she could include her husband. Getting the whole picture of what it is she was about to do, end the whole involvement from that moment on.

The timing was right and she took the opportunity to let him know it's over.

She then broke down and exposed the whole affair to her husband, leaving out the sexual interactions just the affair, for how long and why. She exclaimed it was forced with threats and blackmail. Letting him know that if she didn't, he would take everything she loved and destroy it. Then the only one she would have left was him saying, she would be with him for the rest of her life.

They decided to go to her father and let him know what was going on and ask if he could help with a way out. Her father then informed her of a secret club he has been involved with for many years they were notorious for the import and export of illegal business with China and the Americas. He is part of the hierarchy and sits on the council of decisions.

They meet every three months to go over ¼ year profits and how to approach the next three months business. They have a meeting in the next week, he must attend, and he will bring up this situation for discussion of action. They are not to worry from here on. He said he has all the information he needs and not to consider anything more.

A few weeks later, she had not heard from him and went to her father to inquire. He told her she has nothing to be wondering about he is ghosted. The term ghosted was one his club used when making radicals disappear. People who didn't cooperate with club policy, others who just got in the way or gang members out to create problems such as takeovers, threats of exposure and competition.

The Ghosting

She had given her father the name of him, and with little research, he found his residence. He waited, making sure to learn his routines, for a month. Then during one of his alone times, that would be when he was in intensive downtime meditating and praying. His choice of gods, and her father found this a great irony, was the Buddha.

The little that he had heard, from her manipulation of others and rape; was not part of Buddhism. They found him alone, candles in point, north-south-east-west, on his knees, just as he had directed with her. Caught off guard they surrounded him and put a pillow sack over his head. He was then knocked unconscious with a baseball bat.

Waking, he discovered himself, tied with his arms stretched out and his legs stretched apart and, hanging, two feet off the ground. That's when he entered. He was masked, "So this is how you play. The game is manipulation. I will manipulate your body parts to reconfigure what you look like. In other words, from human to subhuman. And how do we get to subhuman you ask."

Of course, he could not ask anything, his mouth was sewn shut. "Notice you have the freedom of your hands. This is to give you the idea that you have movement. Of course, you do not. The chair beside you is to give height to the person whom you will first encounter. He will begin by tearing off your fingernails. He will then continue by snipping off your fingers one knuckle at a time. He will cauterise each snip with a hot poker. This will continue over the next two days. Then we move to your toes. Again two days of bliss."

He then yelled "come," and a little man walked in.

No bigger than four feet tall. This is your mentor, he is here to teach you about pain, this you will learn over the next week. If you need to talk feel free to call him nemesis. That is who he is to you."

He left and did not return for five days the fifth day was to give him time to rest. Feeding him intravenously kept him alive without having to eat.

He came back and sneeringly said to him "now we will start phase two. But you will rest one more day," he left him to be alone in contemplation. The only people seeing him were the ones changing his intravenous and cleaning the floor around him.

On the seventh day, he came back. "Are you well-rested? Good. We will begin again. This time it will go like this, you will be slowly skinned. It will start with your feet and hands, what's left of them anyway.

He called out "enter," and introduced this next person as retribution, and left.

This person brought with him a table and started setting up several tools, all for cutting and scraping. There were bottles of liquids, unknown to him. But in his mind, he knew it couldn't be good. Retribution started by sectioning all parts, at the joints, with a marker. This took a while, and then he left the room.

Re-entering he went to the table and picked up a scalpel. He then walked over to him and at the ankle cut a line to where his middle toe used to be, and did the same to the underside of his foot sectioning it into two. Surprisingly, it did not hurt but when retribution went to grab the next tool, he knew what he was about to do.

The knife was a tool used for skinning, that's when the pain began. He started at the top of the foot working his way around to the underside. He did this to both feet. His screams went unheard, due to the sewing of his mouth. Retribution then poured some liquid onto a cloth, which he realised later turned out to be iodine, because the pain was so unbearable, he passed out.

All of this was done in silence, except for the muffled screams from his throat. Retribution returned and he was revived, the same then was done to his calves and again he became unconscious. This was done to each section of his body leaving his torso to last, which was done in strips. When retribution was finished, with his torso, he did not return. But when he did:

"Well, you're still alive," he said with enthusiasm. "We have more in store for you but, you will rest for a few days." Not knowing how long he had been hanging there he wondered if there would be any life left, after this, in him. Again the only people he saw were the staff changing his intravenous. It might have been hours, days, weeks but time had escaped him and just as he was regaining his awareness, he walked into the room.

"You must be well-rested," he said slyly. "If you're wondering why we used iodine on your open skin, it was to stop the meat from bleeding. Cauterising the flesh if you can understand what I'm trying to relay to you."

Looking at him in the eyes he could see the terror. The table was left with all the tools needed to carry out the next phase.

"I feel I should explain this next tool as I believe it would interest you. It is used for castrating bulls and, since you have been quit the bull with my daughter, I felt it necessary to use this as a reminder of your interaction with her. Oh, and by the way the woman you shared your experience with, Zyling, she is dead."

Tears began rolling down his face uncontrollably.

"She did not have to endure what you're going through, but then, you are the one who set this in motion. So, here we are. There are two more phases for you. I will do them all myself. We start with the bull," he then walked over and without touching the sack removed his testicles, he passed out again, waking a few days later.

Tying a string around the testacies, while still in the sack, he then placed them around his shoulders and drooped them around his neck.

"You're probably wondering what comes next. Well, this is tricky, 'cause, when the member is removed it has a tendency to haemorrhage. I have to take that into account and make preparations for that. We don't want to lose you. You have to remain conscious for the final phase."

He took a large knife and, unknowing to him, there was a table burner under the cart. He turned it on, it heated up quickly. Putting the knife on it, to get it hot, he also included a second so he could cauterise the wound. After explaining the process to him, he artfully executed the dismemberment of the organ and skilfully cauterised the haemorrhaging. The pain experienced by him was without a doubt excruciating, but he still lived through it.

Upon his awakening, he, the father, was standing right in front of him and couldn't help but feel the presence of something dangling from his mouth. It was his member. There had been just enough of the stitches cut to insert it.

"And now for the final," he said holding the biggest knife ever seen by him.

Starting from the button he began slicing a cut-up through his groin to his torso then into his abdomen, deep, making sure the intestinal tract emptied. Continuing, he cut up above his ribcage and into his neck, slicing his Adam's apple and ended under his chin.

All he could do is watch and, after observing his organs dangling a few inches above the floor, he could see this in full view, as, a mirror had been placed in front of him just before this last phase, he died. It took fifteen minutes, with only one thought going through his head. *"When I get out of this you are all going to die, especially your daughter.*"

He was then dismembered and placed into two oil drums, his head and torso in one and the appendages in the other, added were rocks so they would never resurface.

I was observing this section one day and saw several people on the edge of the brook having a BBQ

"Hey sherry, you okay out there?" Looking over at the island, where the two drums were bottomed, I saw a girl sun bathing, she replied waving back, "Yah." As I watched the girl settle back to sun bathing I noticed him. Right beside her, starring, as that's all he could do, as well he uses his penis as a tongue and brushes it on the skin of the unknown victim. All she feels is a tingling, like a genial brush of a breeze, making her tingle with desire and become wet between her legs. Moaning, that's the only sound he could do, unobserved, except by me. She would hear it as the breeze whispers into her ear.

He would bob, like jumping, to move around; he wanted to lick her, but for the penis tied into place, in his mouth, he could only imagine it. This made him moan because he wanted, really, to kill her.

Ghosted, that's when he feels the most vulnerable because this is what he remembers.

"The last thing to be done," he thought to himself, was to sink the oil drums, with the body pieces, the limbs were separated from the head and torso with two drums, into the depth of Lake Schynstyk at the foot of an island, in the middle of the Lake, called the rock. His ghost remains in suspended agony, on the island, roaming. He cannot leave the Island; he cannot be heard, except in slight breezes and heavy wind, only to be seen by the others haunting these waters.